"W... ...
we should...."

"Shh..." He pressed her close, enfolding her in a hug. "Don't fret, sweetheart. I'm not gonna push you into anything. I'll just hold you, touch you... like one of the horses...."

Stacey pulled back an inch and smiled into his face. "Walker, I'm not one of your horses you can wave a magic wand over, or whatever it is you do to charm them."

"No, you're not a horse," he agreed, grinning. "But if I talk sweet to you, you'll come to me, won't you?"

"Walker..." she said warningly.

He kissed her nose. "Yes, darlin'?"

"Quit." It was a word she'd heard him use with the horses.

"Anything you say." His grin faded, and his expression sobered. "Kiss me again." This was no request, no plea. This was a masculine demand, and Stacey was helpless to refuse.

"Yes," she said. "Yes..."

Dear Reader,

It's May—spring gardens are in full bloom, and in the spirit of the season, we've gathered a special "bouquet" of Silhouette Romance novels for you this month.

Whatever the season, Silhouette Romance novels *always* capture the magic of love with compelling stories that will make you laugh and cry; stories that will move you with the wonder of romance, time and again.

This month, we continue our FABULOUS FATHERS series with Melodie Adams's heartwarming novel, *What About Charlie?* Clint Blackwell might be the local hero when it comes to handling troubled boys, but he never met a rascal like six-year-old Charlie Whitney. And he never met a woman like Charlie's lovely mother, Candace, who stirs up trouble of a different kind in the rugged cowboy's heart.

With drama and emotion, Moyra Tarling takes us to the darker side of love in *Just a Memory Away.* After a serious accident, Alison Montgomery is unable to remember her past. She struggles to learn the truth about her handsome husband, Nick, and a secret about their marriage that might be better left forgotten.

There's a passionate battle of wills brewing in Joleen Daniels's *Inheritance.* The way Jude Emory sees it, beautiful Margret Brolin has stolen the land and inheritance that is rightfully his. How could a man as proud as Jude let her steal his heart as well?

Please join us in welcoming new author Lauryn Chandler who debuts this month with a lighthearted love story, *Mr. Wright.* We're also proud to present *Can't Buy Me Love* by Joan Smith and *Wrangler* by Dorsey Kelley.

In the months to come, watch for books by more of your favorites—Diana Palmer, Suzanne Carey, Elizabeth August, Marie Ferrarella and many more. At Silhouette, we're dedicated to bringing you the love stories you love to read. Our authors and editors want to hear from you. Please write to us; we take our reader comments to heart.

Happy reading!

Anne Canadeo
Senior Editor

WRANGLER
Dorsey Kelley

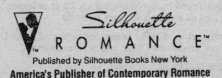

Silhouette
ROMANCE™
Published by Silhouette Books New York
America's Publisher of Contemporary Romance

I'd like to dedicate this book to the many fine organizations helping preserve one of our most precious and beautiful animals: the American mustang.
Among them are: National Mustang Association, Inc.
Institute of Range and the American Mustang
American Mustang & Burro Association, Inc.
Bureau of Land Management, Adopt-A-Horse Program

SILHOUETTE BOOKS
300 East 42nd St., New York, N.Y. 10017

WRANGLER

ISBN: 0-373-08938-4

First Silhouette Books printing May 1993

All the characters in this book have no existence outside the imagination of the author and have no relation whatsoever to anyone bearing the same name or names. They are not even distantly inspired by any individual known or unknown to the author, and all incidents are pure invention.

®: Trademark used under license and registered in the United States Patent and Trademark Office and in other countries.

Printed in the U.S.A.

Books by Dorsey Kelley

Silhouette Romance

Montana Heat #714
Lone Star Man #863
Texas Maverick #900
Wrangler #938

DORSEY KELLEY

claims she has loved and read romance novels forever and can't bear to throw one away. Hence—books stuck into every cranny of her house. Her interests include romping with her three small daughters, tennis and a good bottle of champagne shared with her husband. She lives near the coast in Southern California.

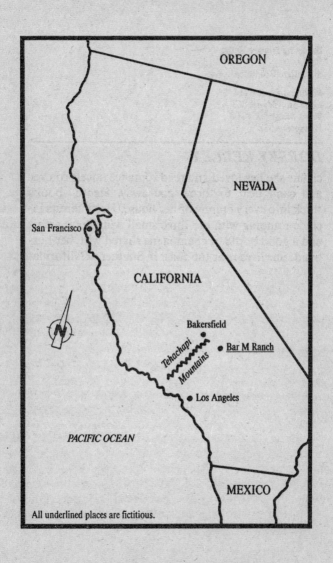

OREGON

NEVADA

San Francisco

CALIFORNIA

Bakersfield

Bar M Ranch

Tehachapi Mountains

Los Angeles

PACIFIC OCEAN

MEXICO

All underlined places are fictitious.

Chapter One

No woman on God's green earth would ever call Wild Horse Walker a handsome man. He knew it—accepted it. But he didn't have to like it. A man didn't need pretty-boy looks to succeed here, only a strong body and a love for ranching. This rugged way of life suited him.

One thing he did have was a way with horses and with ranch work. Cowboyin' was all he knew, all he wanted to know. Mostly, his life was tolerable. It only bothered him on days like this—days when a blue-eyed, nicely rounded guest appeared at the Bar M guest ranch to have a go at riding and relaxing and maybe take one of the better-looking cowboys to her bed.

It was at these times Walker wished his nose hadn't been broken in a ranch accident . . . and looked it. Maybe if his straight slash of midnight-black brows, instead of riding so fiercely across his face, were arched with a welcoming good humor that drew the ladies. Possibly if he smiled more often, instead of wearing his customary scowl, they'd take more notice.

Trouble was, he was angry most of the time. Angry with
the turns his life had taken, the control he'd lost.

A frustrated sound—something that might have been
called a sigh in a more agreeable man—escaped him as he
tightened the cinch of the Appaloosa gelding that the blue-
eyed woman would be taking out on the trail today. He
studied her, wondering if he had a chance. Her chocolate-
brown hair, chin length and shining, made a nice contrast to
the sky-blue color of her eyes; it was an unusual combina-
tion. Sure enough, she stood a little way off, talking and
laughing with one of the other wranglers. This cowboy had
a big smile and an open face, and he got his share of attention from the single female patrons of the dude ranch.

Walker snorted to himself. As good as the other man was
with the ladies, he wasn't much use at roping a thousand-
pound steer or reading the mind of a bull intent on attack.
And he should be, because the Bar M was first and fore-
most a cattle enterprise; the guest ranch had been added to
help support the business.

Shrugging, Walker didn't much mind that he hadn't a
flair for the things the others did. All he really cared about
was the ranch. *His* ranch. At least the Bar M should belong
to him, completely, instead of fifty percent of it going to
that snake, Big Jim Maloney, who'd married Walker's
mother and taken control of the vast acreage of California
ranch lands. His mouth twisted bitterly, and he gave the
cinch a rougher than normal jerk.

Jim ran the Bar M with an iron fist and a whip-sharp
temper. There were no kind words wasted on employees, but
plenty lavished on the paying guests. And to Jim, Walker
was definitely nothing more than an employee.

There was no doubt in Walker's mind that Jim Maloney
had come into his half ownership by underhanded means.
But Walker was determined to get back his rightful share.
Somehow. Some way.

Again his gaze went back to the woman, and his gut tightened with unaccustomed longing. In a soft, quiet way she was beautiful. She appealed to him as few did. A woman like that, he mused, could make a man forget his troubles. . . .

Stacey Maloney stood well back from the corral, away from the big animals inside, and tried to hide her trepidation. She hadn't been on a horse since she was a child growing up in Nebraska, when her grandpa would put her up on his old mare and lead her around the yard. If she was twenty-eight now, that had to be twenty years ago!

She sighed, the memories falling away. She had to be concerned with the future now.

And now was a good time to take a vacation, what with the architectural firm she'd worked for as a secretary declaring Chapter Eleven and leaving her unemployed. Besides, Jim Maloney, her father-in-law, had been adamant. "It's high time I got to know my grandson," he'd practically shouted over the phone.

Stacey passed a hand over her forehead at the memory of his booming voice, mussing her straight fringe of dark hair as she did so. Jim had called repeatedly in the months since seeing her at Dennis's funeral, asking for Stacey and her son to visit. It had just happened that this last time Jim had called on the same day she'd discovered she was out of a job.

And now they were here. With almost as much wariness as she eyed the horses, she let her gaze scan the tall wrangler leading the brown-spotted Appaloosa toward her. She knew the man had been watching her, and his frankly interested stare made her feel slightly uneasy. He wore faded blue jeans and a long-sleeved shirt with a tear in one sleeve in an even more faded blue. His rawhide-brown Stetson was pulled aggressively low over his dark brow, and his mouth was firmly set in a frown. Stacey couldn't imagine the stern man ever smiling.

Still, she tried a tentative smile of her own as he came to a halt beside her. "Hi," she said, her voice not trembling at all despite her deep misgivings. She wasn't going to let her son down by chickening out now. She would ride the horse. "Uh, do you think you could help me up?" Transforming her friendly expression into an apologetic one, she made a gesture toward the patiently waiting gelding. "It's been years since I've been on a horse, and I don't think—"

"The mounting block's over there," he cut in, pointing at a set of steps that led up to a platform, from which other riders were climbing onto their mounts.

"Oh, of course," she said, letting her feet drag as she went to climb the steps. At the top she waited awkwardly for the wrangler to lead her horse over. He did so without comment.

"Come on, Mom," her son called from atop his own mount, a bay-colored horse. "Everybody's ready to go."

"I'm coming, Geoff," Stacey assured the boy. He sounded like a normal, impatient ten-year-old instead of the subdued child he'd become, and she was glad of the eager note in his voice. It took no more than a quick survey of the corral to see that Geoff was right. The dozen or so other guests were all mounted and waiting for her. She'd procrastinated long enough.

Drawing a calming breath, she put a tentative hand on the saddle horn and tucked her foot into the stirrup. The darn horse was so—so big, and it was such a long way to the ground. What if she fell off? What if she—

"You'll need the reins, darlin'," the cowboy said from his post at the horse's head.

Darlin'! Stacey glanced sharply at the man and met his steady gaze. Beneath the brown Stetson his eyes were green, dark fringed and clear—definitely his best feature. Fleetingly she noticed a bump on the bridge of his nose and wondered how he'd gotten it.

But in his eyes she found no improper suggestion. She decided to let the *darlin'* slide. Taking the leather reins into her left fist, she swung her right leg over the horse and landed with a small thump in the middle of the animal's back.

The horse immediately started walking briskly toward the open gate, where the other riders were filing out. Stacey's eyes widened. Now what? The confounded beast would escape out that opening and take off with her, probably at a thundering gallop! If only she hadn't capitulated when Geoff had begged they take the two weeks she'd allocated as vacation time to visit his grandfather's ranch. She had a little money saved. They could have been in Hawaii right now, wearing bathing suits and basking in the sun. They could have rented a mountain cabin and fished serenely off a nice dock. They could have stayed home and cleaned out closets!

Casting a baleful eye at her towheaded son, Stacey felt some of her initial fear and reluctance fade. Geoff had eagerly taken the lead in the procession, guiding his horse as he'd been taught in the saddle camp he'd attended earlier this summer. He was bombarding one of their guides, the stern-faced wrangler, with questions about everything to do with horse care and riding. And her own mount hadn't yet taken off with her, but strode calmly along with his nose half-buried in the tail of the next horse.

Since their arrival an hour before, Stacey hadn't seen Jim Maloney. She'd only gotten his note, urging her to take advantage of the afternoon ride. It was odd. She'd been a Maloney for nearly ten years—married to Jim's son—but she'd only met her own father-in-law once. Ironically, at her husband's funeral. Dennis had been estranged from his father and had never spoken about him except to say that a colder son of a gun had never lived.

But then, Dennis hadn't turned out to be terribly warm, either.

All at once Stacey felt guilty. Dennis had been a steady husband. He just hadn't been demonstrative. Or particularly affectionate. In fact, he wasn't affectionate at all. And she'd tried so hard to please him, to be the wife he wanted. Yet she'd always sensed that the harder she tried, the less he appreciated her. But he was gone now. Gone forever.

She couldn't see herself marrying again. But if by some chance she did, she decided, as their procession wound through yellow-tipped sagebrush and into the meadow of a huge valley, it would be to a smiling, lighthearted man. Someone who was affectionate, someone who'd talk to her, bring her flowers, tell her she was pretty. He'd do all the frivolous things men did for the women with whom they were crazy in love.

A sudden smile sprang to Stacey's mouth. Of all the absurd fantasies, imagining there was such a man anywhere in the world!

Still smiling, her gaze inexplicably drifted to the curt cowboy who'd called her *darlin'*. In shock, she realized he had twisted around in the saddle of his gray horse and was already looking at her. He'd caught that silly grin on her face!

"You doing okay, honey?" His eyes touched her hands, inexpertly clasping the reins, dipped to her jean-clad thighs, then rose with excruciating slowness to rest for a second on the curve of her breasts.

Stacey flushed. There he went with another endearment. And those bold eyes! "No problem at all." She lifted her chin. "In fact, I'm doing so well, you might have to put me on the payroll soon."

Something resembling a grin lifted one corner of his mouth. "That we might." Turning back, he resumed his conversation with her son as if nothing at all had happened.

Glaring at his broad back, Stacey firmed her lips, tempted to report the insolent man to Jim. Undoubtedly he wouldn't want his cowboys offending the lady guests of the ranch.

But after a moment she took a deep breath and felt her flush fade. She'd never in her life been a snitch; she wouldn't start now. The cowboy with the broken nose could stare at her all he liked—next time she wouldn't flinch.

Besides, she hadn't come here to make trouble for the employees or complain to the boss. She'd come for a much-needed rest and to decide what she'd do with her life. And for Geoff. He wasn't doing well in school. He'd always been a quiet child, but lately, in the year since her husband's death, Geoff had grown even quieter. The only thing that had truly animated him lately was the prospect of coming to "a real ranch."

Geoff was introverted and pale. She worried about him. He didn't make friends easily, didn't play with other kids much. His reading skills were excellent, but Stacey felt he spent far more time buried in the pages of his Western storybooks than was normal.

"Look!" Geoff's excited shout startled her so much, she had to make a grab for the saddle horn. Her son pointed to one side, away from the trail they were following, down into the huge, spreading valley. The lead rider stopped his horse, and the others came to a halt.

"What is it, Geoff?" Stacey kept a careful hand on the horn.

"Don't you see 'em, Mom? Don't you see the horses?"

"Horses?" she asked, shading her eyes and squinting into the distance. Tiny dots moved across the valley, slowly transforming into creatures with manes and tails.

"Are they wild, Walker?" Geoff, practically bouncing in his saddle, asked the wrangler with the crooked nose.

"Yep." The cowboy pinched off the end of a long blade of grass and chewed on it. "Wild as jackrabbits."

Geoff's eyes were wide. "Wow," he breathed. "Are they...like mustangs?"

Walker nodded and urged the group forward again. "They're escaped saddle stock, some born on the range, some older scruffy rag tails. And yes, there are a small bunch of mustangs. We let 'em run free, long as their numbers stay down."

"Wow," Geoff said again, and Stacey smiled. He was at the limit of his vocabulary to show he was impressed. Then he pointed again. "Look at that red one. He looks pretty nice."

Twisting in the saddle, Walker glanced back. Stacey followed his gaze to the long-legged horse standing proudly between them and his band of mares. The animal was sorrel red, his coat gleaming in the bright sunlight. He wore four perfect white stockings and a blaze of white on his forehead.

"That's a young stallion we bought a couple years ago for breeding," Walker said. "But he's not nice. He's rank. An outlaw. When he jumped the pasture fence, we let him go. Out there, at least, he's producing a good colt crop every year."

Up ahead the other guide broke into song while the boy gazed wistfully at the sorrel stallion. Walker grinned wryly to himself. Another horse-crazy kid. He'd been one himself twenty years ago. He guessed it was something he'd never outgrown.

Behind him he heard the plodding hoofbeats of the gentle Appaloosa he'd assigned to the blue-eyed woman and turned again to check on her. She wore new, artificially faded jeans, a plain woven cloth belt and a simple, but unWesternlike blouse with some kind of ruffle at the neckline. If she supposed she was hiding the generous swell of her breasts, she was mistaken, he thought, letting his gaze linger there. Her horse stumbled over a rock, and she grabbed for the saddle leather again. A true greenhorn. But

her rounded bosom gave a soft bounce, and Walker grinned.
No, sir, she was hiding exactly nothing.

She looked up at him, caught him staring, and he was
struck by the beauty of her huge eyes. They reflected an
openness that somehow drew him.

Still grinning, he realized he definitely liked what he saw.

He reined in his horse, dropping back until he rode beside her. "What's your name, honey?" he asked in a low
voice. The other riders moved ahead several steps, and the
guide's twanging song about his lost love enthralled them.
Walker and the woman were virtually alone.

"I'm Stacey," she returned. "You're . . . Walker?"

"Walker Marshall. Pleased to meet you." He smiled,
showing all his teeth, and was gratified when she smiled
back shyly. Perhaps he might get lucky with this one, despite his flawed face. Her allure was understated, not bla-
tant like that of most of the girls the others went after.
Maybe they'd skip this one and Walker could . . .

"That's my son, Geoff." She nodded at the eager boy.

"That right?"

"Yes. He just loves horses. He's been begging for months
to visit a real ranch."

"You came to the right place. How long're you staying?"

"Two full weeks."

Two weeks. It should be plenty long enough. He let his
gaze have free rein now as he studied her. She sat in her
saddle gingerly, as if she was afraid she might topple over
any second. That was okay. In two weeks maybe he'd teach
her to ride properly. And teach her a few other things, as
well.

Walker shook his head and forced his eyes away, so he
could do his job and check on the other dudes. They were
all fine, and he turned again to Stacey. It was unprece-
dented, he thought with some surprise, for this attraction to
a woman to build so fast. Never before had he known so

quickly that he wanted one in particular. Perhaps it had something to do with the vulnerability he thought he glimpsed in her.

For some reason the idea made him uneasy.

She was talking, her voice a pleasing contralto that soothed and excited him at the same time. He had to make himself listen to her words.

"... I'm really not a ranch-vacation type of person. Swimming pools and palm trees and drinks with little umbrellas in them are more my style." She gave a self-deprecating laugh. "But Geoff had his heart set. So when Jim called and invited us, why, naturally I couldn't—"

"What?" Something clicked in Walker's mind, freezing the pleasantly predatory feelings he'd felt growing for the woman. Grabbing her horse's bridle, he brought it to a sudden halt. "You said your name is Stacey?"

"Why... yes. But—"

"Stacey what?"

"Maloney. I'm...I am—was Jim's daughter-in-law. I was married to Dennis. Did...did you know him?"

Walker spat out an earthy epithet and glared at her. "You were Dennis's wife! I should have realized you'd come around someday." For several seconds he stared at her pretty face, wishing bitterly she were anybody else. Anybody in the world but Dennis Maloney's widow. He missed Dennis. Although they'd been nothing alike, Dennis had been his boyhood companion. But then Dennis had abandoned the ranch, and soon after married this woman.

In her eyes he detected confusion and bewilderment. The innocent act suited her, he decided, his anger rising again. Because, of course, it was an act.

He didn't even bother accusing her on that score, but cut right to the heart of the matter. "Don't for a second think you can move in on my territory."

"What—what territory—?"

"This ranch is *mine*," he went on grimly. "Do you hear? Or it will be. Just because you got lucky enough to marry the old man's son doesn't mean you'll get ownership. When all's said and done, I'll end up with this operation, no one else!"

With that he let go of her bridle and spurred his horse ahead. He couldn't bear to look at her anymore. She had a kid—Jim's *grandson!* The threat was real now.

"Wait! What are you talking about? I'm not after ownership of this place." She tried, unsuccessfully, to get her horse to speed up and catch him. But over his shoulder he could plainly see that she hadn't the faintest idea of how to go about it. Her mount continued to move forward at a shambling walk. Walker smiled without humor. If the gold digger wanted her name on the grant deed of a working ranch, she ought to know how to handle a horse.

Wheeling his horse, he kept his voice low so the others ahead wouldn't hear. "You don't know about me, do you, honey? Well, I'm the fly in the soup for you. I'm Maloney's stepson. Surprised?"

"Well," she sputtered. "Frankly, yes. I didn't know Dennis *had* a stepbrother. Were you at the funeral?"

"Yeah, I was there for a few minutes."

"Oh. I . . . didn't see you. There were so many people."

"You're probably wondering why it's so important to me to own one hundred percent of this place." He grinned at her wolfishily. "I'll tell you. It's because this spread belonged to my mother. She inherited it from her family. Now that she's gone, it's rightfully mine, not that bastard, Jim Maloney's!"

Stacey's mount grew restive, wanting to be off after the other horses. When she couldn't stop it, Walker grabbed the bridle again. This time he leaned close, until he knew he had her full attention. "When my mother married Jim, he had nothing. Now he's a wealthy man. You look like a bright woman, Stacey. Figure it out."

She stared at him. "Figure what out?"

"I can't prove it, maybe I never will. But I know, as surely as I know this mountain range that as soon as Maloney got himself named as the sole beneficiary of my mother's will, he as good as killed her."

Chapter Two

Stacey stared at the cowboy in shock. "Jim...Jim *killed* your mother?" She clutched at the leather reins.

Walker looked away, his face tight and tense. "I said 'as good as killed her.'" For several seconds he said nothing more, merely staring toward the wild horses. But she was sure he saw little; the man was looking inward. When he resumed talking, his voice was rushed and low. "He was never good for her. Too forceful, too abrupt. She was gentle...kind. He walked all over her." The muscles of his jaw worked. "I still don't understand why she married him."

Carefully, Stacey asked, "What...exactly did she die of?"

"They called it cancer." He swung around to meet her gaze, and she almost recoiled from the anger, the anguish deep in his eyes. "I say despair."

Despite Walker's obvious pain, Stacey was loath to let the subject drop. He'd made some pretty strong accusations about Jim. The other riders were perhaps fifty yards down the trail now, the horses slowly making their way through the sage. She asked, "What reason could there possibly be

for Jim to want your mother dead?'' Instantly, she winced
at her own wording. Hurrying, she added, ''I mean, you
mentioned she was a gentle, kind person.''

''As I said, Jim had nothing when he married her. She
owned this thirty-thousand-acre ranch. It's clear, isn't it?''

Stacey hesitated. She didn't want to say, ''No, it isn't,''
when Walker's mood was so uncertain. She wasn't at all sure
the unpredictable man wouldn't explode if he was goaded
too far.

Instead, she decided to take another tack. Dennis had
never mentioned his stepbrother to her—as if Walker, along
with the rest of his family, didn't exist. So she wondered if
the two brothers' relationship would reveal something.
''You must have been about the same age as Dennis—so you
grew up together?'' At his curt nod, she asked, ''How did
you get along?''

He shrugged tightly. ''We got along. He liked reading and
hanging around inside. I was always outdoors playing, and
later, working the ranch.'' Seeming to catch himself, he
stopped. ''Why do you want to know?''

She shrugged with more bravado than she felt. ''Dennis
was my husband, the father of my son. It's natural I want
to learn about him. For Geoff's sake.''

He seemed to accept that. Glancing at the others, he finally released her horse's bridle and leaned toward her, some
of the menace in his manner returning. ''You want to know
things, huh? Well, my mother left this place to Jim because
she figured he'd take care of Dennis and me. What a joke.''

''You're still here, aren't you?'' she blurted recklessly.

Narrowed green eyes bored into hers. ''Sure, darlin','' he
drawled softly. ''I'm still here. It's something for you to remember.''

She swallowed but kept her features composed. ''At the
risk of repeating myself, let me reassure you that I have no
designs on this ranch. I'm city bred and raised, and I like it
there. You've nothing to fear from me.''

"You think I'm scared?"

Inwardly, Stacey sighed. Now this difficult man thought she was questioning his masculinity. Lord save her from male egos! "No, I—"

"You don't worry about me. Besides, you have no right to this place. None at all."

"But I don't—"

"No? Then what did you come for?"

Stacey ground her teeth. "I told you. To visit."

The most thoroughly skeptical expression she'd ever seen settled over Walker's face. "Right. And when your two weeks are up, you'll take off and we'll never see you again?"

She shifted in her saddle. The arrogance of the man was beginning to get to her. He'd shown no courtesy, nothing but an antagonism that she didn't deserve. He'd made her feel unwelcome and uncomfortable, and on the heels of such thoughts, she felt a sudden, uncharacteristic urge to nettle him, just a little. "Maybe we'll come back in the fall for another visit. Maybe we'll come back regularly. Does that bother you?"

He snorted. "You couldn't bother me if you tried." He wheeled his horse abruptly and cantered away. Back at the group he rode up and down the line of guests, inquiring politely how each was enjoying the ride. Stacey watched, irritated with herself for stooping to taunt him. It wasn't like her at all, and she could only lay the blame at Walker's booted feet.

It appeared that today he'd brought out the worst in her. As her horse shuffled a fraction faster to catch up, she lifted her chin and drew a bracing breath. Well, she'd always been a congenial person. Lots of people liked her, she reassured herself. Eventually, when Walker came to realize she posed no real threat, he'd like her, too. She was sure of it.

James Patrick Maloney barreled into the house like a stock truck plowing down tumbleweeds. "Stacey, honey!"

he bellowed, scooping her into his embrace and giving her
a rib-crushing hug. He set her down. The early evening
sunset filtering in from the ranch house's huge front windows glinted on his mane of white hair. "Glad to see you,
even if it is ten or eleven years late. Where's the boy? I want
to meet that grandson of mine." He put hamlike hands on
his hips and swung around, surveying the living room.

Stacey looked up at least a foot. He had to be a good six
foot four. And probably weighed in at two-thirty, she
guessed, judging by his expansive girth. With her palm, she
took a surreptitious inventory of her ribs and decided none
were cracked. "Uh, Geoff is upstairs, showering. We took
your advice and went on the afternoon ride. He'll be right
down."

"Good! Good!" He headed across the room to wedge
himself behind a small oak wet bar and tossed ice cubes into
two old-fashioned glasses. "Waited this long, guess a few
more minutes won't hurt. Meantime we'll have a little ton-
sil varnish and talk, eh?" From beneath the oak bar he
produced a bottle of Kentucky whiskey and poured out lib-
eral doses.

Stacey liked the informal feel of the main house, all done
in a homey, Southwestern decor. Earth-toned Indian-print
throws and country accents like bleached cow skulls and
horseshoe sculptures dotted the room.

Since the kitchen was just off the living room, comfort-
ing smells of baking bread and roasting chicken wafted
through.

Walker sauntered in, hung his Stetson on a rack and
nodded toward the glasses. "Got any more of that?"

Jim lifted one burly shoulder. "Get it yourself."

Walker's customary frown deepened, and Stacey wondered at Jim's tone. Unobtrusively she studied Walker. He
wore the same clothes as this morning, the dusty jeans and
torn shirt clearly faded by wear and repeated washings. As
a concession to the day's heat, he'd rolled up his sleeves to

his elbows, revealing muscular forearms, their undersides crossed by thick veins—a testament to lifelong physical labor. Now that he'd shed his hat, she could see his hair was thick, a deep brown and glossy. His eyes still expressed the same intensity, and when they met hers, she instantly felt some of her earlier edginess return.

Jim was talking. "...and you're to make yourself at home here, Stace. *Mi casa es su casa,* got it? Everything I got's yours."

In the background Walker made a strangled noise, and Stacey glanced at him.

But Jim drew her attention again. "Now how'd you like the trail ride? Walker give you a good horse?"

She accepted the glass shoved unceremoniously into her hand and took a small sip. "Uh, why, yes, Spot was just—"

"Spot!" Jim swung around to confront Walker. "You gave her that plug? What's gotten into you, boy? Why didn't you put her up on Bosco or Mustache?"

"Because—" Walker poured a hefty dose of the whiskey into a glass "—Bosco or Mustache would've left her on her rump in the dirt. Somehow I don't think you'd have been so happy about that."

"It's part of your job to match guests to horses, and any fool would know I don't want my daughter-in-law up on that lazy cayuse, Spot."

"I'm doing my job by matching your *daughter-in-law*—" he emphasized the title with a hard glance at Stacey "—with a horse she can stay on. If you'd have seen—"

"Please." Stacey held her free hand in the air. "Don't argue on my account. I'm sure Walker was right to match me with a calm animal. I'm afraid I'm not much of a rider." She smiled apologetically at Jim, hoping for peace between the two.

Jim glared at the younger man for a long moment, then turned back to Stacey, his manner gentling. "That's fine, Stace. If you like old Spot, you can ride him all you want."

At that moment Geoff appeared in the doorway, his blond hair still damp but carefully combed behind his ears. "And can I ride Skipper all I want, too?"

"Of course you can," Jim boomed, a grin appearing on his face. "You're my grandson, aren't you? Well, you do just any damn—darn thing you want while you're on this ranch. Now come here and let me look at you."

He hunkered down and gestured Geoff over. After a questioning glance at his mother, the boy walked slowly toward the strange man. Jim held out his huge paw, and Geoff stared at the expanse of palm before gingerly allowing his smaller one to be swallowed up. "Wow, mister, you have a big hand."

Jim threw back his head and guffawed. "That I do, son, that I do. I'm big all the way around. And you're too scrawny. But we'll fatten you up quick here at the Bar M." He stood up.

"But I don't want to get fat."

Jim laughed harder, and Stacey smiled. She thought she even caught a glimpse of humor in Walker's expression, but it was gone too fast for her to be sure. To her son she said, "You won't get fat, I promise. And don't call your grandfather mister."

"How about Grandpa?" Jim suggested. "I like the sound of it."

"Okay." The boy clambered onto a cowhide bar stool and sat on his knees. "Grandpa, you won't believe what we saw today! Wild horses. Walker says there's even some mustangs!"

"So," Jim said with a snort, "Wild Horse Walker's been at it again, huh?"

Geoff looked as confused as Stacey felt. She said, "Wild Horse Walker?"

"That's what we call him hereabouts." Carelessly Jim threw a handful of peanuts from a silver bowl into his mouth, and Stacey noted Walker's guarded expression. "He's crazy about the broom tails, even if they are worthless."

Curiously, Walker said nothing.

"But today I saw a great one," Geoff put in. "It was dark reddish brown and had white on its legs. It didn't look bad."

"Now *that* horse isn't a mustang. I bought that stallion a few years back for breeding. He comes from real good quarter horse stock. But he was hard to handle. Somehow he got out. Somebody *accidentally* left the gate open." He sent an accusatory glare toward Walker, who remained mute.

Again Stacey felt the need to intervene. Somebody needed to take a firm hold of the conversational reins. "That's unfortunate, Jim, but both Geoff and I want you to know how grateful we are that you've invited us here. We could use a vacation, and just coincidentally, Geoff's been begging to go on a ranch trip. In fact, we've only been here a few hours, and I haven't seen him this happy since—"

She'd been about to say, "Since before Dennis passed away," but caught herself. "Well . . . for some time."

"Good!" Jim boomed. "Glad you're here. Now, I'm starved. Miriam's dinner should be ready about now."

Walker set down his empty whiskey glass. "I'm going to check on the new foal."

Ignoring Walker, Jim ushere   tacey and Geoff toward the dining room. Over her shoulder Stacey watched Walker collect his hat, jam it on and stride out the front door, his boots clumping on the hardwood flooring. "Isn't Walker going to eat with us?" she asked.

"Naw, he'll get something later. He's not the sociable type, anyway. He doesn't like to join in."

At the doorway Stacey paused, letting Jim and Geoff go inside and greet the other guests waiting to be served Mir-

iam's roast-chicken dinner. Out the front window she saw
Walker head down the steps toward the big barn. His Stetson was cocked over one eye, his gait was loose-limbed and
slightly arrogant. Although she was sure she must have been
visible to him from her post by the window, he never once
looked up. Never once acknowledged her.

Dinner was a congenial affair, with the dozen-odd guests
making interesting companions. There were three or four
children fairly close to Geoff's age, yet he stayed near
Stacey, only shyly glancing at the other kids. Jim held court
at the head, telling loud, outrageous tales of cowboying in
his younger days—of Wyoming winters that froze not only
the water tanks but the cattle standing in their tracks. The
guests loved it, and Stacey noticed Geoff was enthralled.

Afterward they retired to the room they shared, and she
fell into a deep sleep, only to be awakened what seemed
minutes later by Geoff. "Mom." He shook her shoulder.
"Mom, you gotta get up. The sun's coming over the mountain—we'll miss the morning ride!"

Opening one eye, Stacey peered at the bedside clock.
"Geoff, it's five a.m.! The morning ride's not until nine-
thirty."

"Oh." He sat on the side of her twin bed, and his smile
was chagrined. "Sorry." She noticed in the dim light that he
was fully dressed even down to his denim jacket and new
cowboy boots. "But can I go to the barn and wait? Grandpa
said I could do anything I want."

Groggy, Stacey got up on one elbow and rubbed her eyes.
"Geoff, are you going to wait down there four and a half
hours? Come on, even you need breakfast, and that's not
served until seven. Besides, how do we know anyone else is
up?"

"Walker said he'd be up early. He said horse wranglers
got to get up with the sun." He waited expectantly.

"All right—"

"Yahoo!" The boy bounded off the bed and was halfway to the door before Stacey could stop him.

"Just a minute, young man. You can go to the barn if you promise not to get in anybody's way."

"I won't."

"And absolutely don't go near the horses, you understand? Wait for the cowboys to...er...do whatever they do with them."

"I will."

"And mind your manners. You—" But she was talking to thin air. Geoff had slipped out, and she could hear the patter of his size five feet on the wooden floor. Smiling, she guessed she'd as soon try to lasso the wind as keep Geoff inside at the ranch. It was good. Too long inside, too bookish, he needed fresh air and physical exercise.

Sitting up, she swung her legs over the rose-colored quilt and put her feet on the oak floor. As they touched the cool wood, her toes instantly curled up and she shivered.

Forcing herself to dress quickly in blue jeans, a longsleeved flannel shirt and scuffed black flats, Stacey ruefully took in her appearance in the bedroom's full-length mirror. Yesterday she'd discovered her clothes were ill suited to ranch life. All the other guests, from the older women to the smallest child, sported cowboy boots. Some had fancy handtooled belts and felt hats.

Chuckling, she guessed any self-respecting cowboy—like Walker—would spot her as a true city slicker from a country mile. That was fine, she reassured herself. She hadn't the budget for boots and belts and such—not for just a two-week stay—and impressing any cowboys in the vicinity was extremely low on her list of priorities. Especially Walker.

What she really should be thinking about was her future. The hard fact was that she needed a job. Her limited savings account wouldn't hold out for long. Unfortunately, she couldn't go to her mother for a loan—not that she wanted to. Widowed herself for many years, Stacey's mother had just now, finally, found a man she could love and gotten married again. The new couple cared for each other deeply, but had little money to spare.

Sighing, she brushed her hair and applied mascara, then went in search of the kitchen and coffee. Even at this early hour the house was coming alive. She passed several rooms and peeked into one with an open door. Apparently it was Jim's office, as it contained a desk and computer, filing cabinets and a leather sofa.

Should she go to an employment agency and look for another position as bookkeeper for an architectural firm? She knew a good deal about the business—Dennis had been an architect. Or should she perhaps go for something different? After years in the industry, her interest had waned, and her bookkeeping had grown stale. Eyeing the computer, she chewed her lip. Perhaps she could go to night school and become a computer programmer.

"Mom! Come on." Geoff was at her side, tugging her hand. "You got to come see the neat stuff in the barn. They got goats and sheeps and even this teeny-weeny horse that's so little you can't even ride him."

"Sheep," she corrected, smiling, allowing herself to be towed along. "Not sheeps."

"Yeah, right." They were approaching the front door now, passing the dining room, when Stacey smelled fragrant muffins and frying bacon. Miriam, an aproned, fiftyish woman hired as cook, bustled from the kitchen to the dining room, setting covered metal pans of eggs and ham over electric heaters. Spotting Stacey, the woman paused to tuck a bit of her graying hair back into her bun and smiled, the lines in her face creasing kindly.

Bent on his mission, Geoff continued pulling Stacey right past, and she glanced wistfully at the warm coffee cake on the sideboard.

"Uh, Geoff, how about if we grab a quick muffin—"

"Mom, you won't believe all the horses they got!" He pressed on as if not hearing. "And Walker says every morning I can help get them ready." He stopped when they were halfway to the barn. Puffing himself up, he thumbed his thin chest. "Walker says now that I'm doing man's work, I'm a junior wrangler."

Stacey smiled at his beaming face. Her stomach rumbled, but she ignored it. Seeing her son so enthusiastic about this place—about anything—did her heart good. She guessed food could wait.

Outside, the late-spring air had a distinct snap, yet Stacey was comfortable in her flannel shirt and jeans. Clean mountain sunshine poured down, making her squint. She didn't mind.

At the barn only one man was working to curry the horses and saddle them. Walker went about his business with a methodical thoroughness Stacey could only admire. She perched a safe distance from the big animals and watched while Geoff chattered. Walker ignored her. Or perhaps he was too busy for small talk, she told herself, willing to overlook his rudeness. After all, she had made up her mind that they would become friends. She was sure they'd like each other if given a chance.

In the big corral Walker slowly approached the mount he wanted with a halter and lead rope. He wore faded jeans with a leather belt and gold buckle etched with a bucking horse, a blue chambray work shirt and his dark Stetson. His skin, she noticed again, was burned a deep brown, and his black brows still slanted over his eyes in that perpetual scowl.

Watching him whisper into a buckskin gelding's ear, she saw the animal, at first restive, grow calm at Walker's soothing voice and touch. She realized he had a fine skill with horses.

Speaking softly, he easily caught a palomino and led it to a hitching post for saddling. With practiced hands he ad-

justed the blanket, making sure there was none bunched up,
"So it won't irritate the horse's back," Geoff told her in
hushed tones. Then Walker partially removed the halter and
bridled the horse, slipping the curb bit between its teeth.

"Curb bits are Western," Geoff explained seriously.
"Snaffles are English."

"I see." Stacey ruffled his hair. "You sure have learned a
lot in a short time. I guess junior wranglers need to know
everything about horses."

"Yeah." He skipped happily toward the barn with a
promise to round up as many goats as he could find.

When the last horse was saddled and safely tied to the
corral fence, Walker turned and strode directly toward
Stacey. She watched him approach, her eyes wary.

He rested one hand on the post beside her thigh. "Morn-
in', Miz Maloney," Walker drawled, halting at her knee. He
had to look up at her since she was still on the fence. His
fingers were lean and as brown as his face. Strong. She
didn't know why, but the proximity of his hand to her leg
made her nervous. He smiled. "Sleep well?"

Was he going to be nice today?

"Well, yes, actually, I did. Until my—er—junior wrangler woke me at dawn." She could be nice, too. "Did you
sleep well?"

Politely she waited for his answer; it was long in coming.
Walker hadn't once glanced away, but merely stood studying her face with an unblinking intensity. His green eyes,
attractively fringed with black lashes, held mysterious inner thoughts she couldn't begin to fathom.

He thumbed his hat onto the back of his head, as if he
wanted to get an even better look at her. Then, surprising
her, he clamped hard hands around her waist and lifted her
off the rail. To keep her balance she clutched at his shoulders. They were sturdy and muscular and warm.

"You want to know how I slept?" Walker asked in a low,
husky voice when she was on the ground. "Truth is, there's

a lot on my mind." His gaze dipped to her breasts for an interminable second. "I got a feelin' that as long as you're here, I won't get much rest."

Acting nonchalant was incredibly difficult, when his palms were still encircling her vulnerable waist. The cloth of her thin shirt felt nonexistent, as if his hands were really on her bare skin. "Then I'm sorry if I've disturbed you," she got out, her voice ridiculously breathy. "You know, you have nothing to be concerned about."

"I don't, huh?" His gaze dropped again.

Belatedly gathering her wits, Stacey nervously stepped away from him. His arms dropped to his sides and hung there. His gaze remained riveted to hers; it almost felt as if he were still touching her.

"Hey, Walker." Geoff materialized in the small space between them, his fingers stuffed under the collar of a small white goat. "Where'd you get that bump on your nose?"

"Geoff!" Stacey was mortified by her son's breach of good manners.

"It's all right." Walker crouched beside the boy, and Stacey was relieved she was no longer the focus of his attention; he had a way of unsettling her. He smiled at the child. "I was close to your age, maybe a coupla' years older. We boys decided to hold our own private rodeo, right here in this corral. Well, I was a cocky kid, and I figured I could ride Jim's biggest bull."

Stacey gasped. "At twelve years old you got on a bull?"

He nodded. "Maybe thirteen. A Hereford-Brahman cross. Mean, too. Anyway, I lived to regret it." Touching the bump on the bridge of his nose, he grinned. "I lasted all of two jumps when that nasty old bull really got mad and tossed me into this here fence. Fact, I think that notch right there is where my face kissed this post. See it?"

Geoff leaned over, eyes wide with awe. "Wow."

Stacey crossed her arms skeptically. "That two-by-two-inch notch, huh?"

His mouth kicked up at one corner. "Well, maybe it is this smaller one."

"No." Geoff shook his head emphatically, staring at the scarred wood. "It's this big one, I bet."

The cowboy chuckled, straightening, and Stacey laughed with him. It was amazing, she thought, what a smile could do to his otherwise fierce features. His eyes lighted up and crinkled at the corners. Against the weathered canvas of his face, his teeth were straight and brilliantly white. As her laughter died, Stacey found herself staring at him with something close to awe. The man was quite devastating when he deigned to smile.

Forty yards off a truck engine roared to life, and they turned. Jim sent the vehicle into drive, and his back tires sprayed gravel onto the dirt road as he headed away from the ranch.

"There he goes again," Walker muttered.

"What?" Stacey asked.

"Nothing. It's just . . . nothing." His smile vanished.

Stacey caught at his arm; it seemed important for her to know. "Tell me. Where's Jim going?"

He looked at her, his brows coming down. "You sure are inquisitive for just being here on a visit." He shook her off, and his frown turned into a glower. "Truth is, I don't know where he goes. He doesn't talk to me much. And usually I don't pry into his comings and goings. But I'm going to make it my business to notice yours, Miz Maloney." He smiled again, but this time it didn't seem to include his eyes.

Confused, Stacey gasped at his sudden attack, and felt a painful flush rush into her cheeks.

He went right on. "While you're here on the Bar M, I'll be keeping my eye on you."

Chapter Three

Walker appeared for dinner that evening, surprising Stacey, who'd thought he never ate with the guests. But at six o'clock sharp he was in the dining room, standing behind a chair at Jim's right. Immediately Stacey was on guard. His words from that afternoon still rang in her ears. He'd promised to "keep an eye on her," and here he was, doing it!

Jim spotted her lingering behind other ranch guests in the doorway and motioned to her and Geoff to take the chairs at his left. "Come in," he boomed. "Let's eat."

Still standing, Walker watched her, his features set in sardonic lines. She glared at him, but he merely tipped his head, as if agreeing she should sit.

When she and Geoff took their places, her son accepted an enormous plateful, piled high with roast beef, browned potatoes and broccoli covered with cheese sauce. But the boy ignored the food at first, leaning across Stacey toward Jim. "Grandpa," he began eagerly, "can I go out tomorrow on the trail ride? Maybe I'll see that wild horse again."

"Sure, boy, sure. The wrangler here'll take the whole group over that way, won't you, Walker?"

Walker chewed a forkful of beef, his expression reserved. Hatless, he had combed his thick hair away from his forehead, and under the lamp that hung over the long table, his tan looked dark and attractive. "I'll take the group that way," he said.

A few of the other guests who hadn't seen the wild horses the day before expressed interest. Geoff said, "You'll come, won't you, Mom?"

Stacey glanced up, and for some reason her gaze collided with Walker's. He was staring at her. "Uh, no, I'm a little sore from yesterday's ride."

"You'll get over that," Jim pronounced. "Besides, those mustangs are scruffy stock. Don't know why anybody wants to look at 'em, anyway. Ask me, I say we round them all up and let the Bureau of Land Management handle them."

"The BLM," Walker informed his stepfather stiffly, "has almost more horses now than they can manage. You just leave them where they are, they're not hurting anything." He resumed eating.

Jim looked at Walker sourly. "The hell they're not. They don't profit anyone."

"Begging your pardon." A fortyish man, wearing new, store-bought Western clothes, including a purple bandanna tied dashingly around his neck, raised his voice. "It's none of my business, Jim, it's your ranch. But I think they do profit us. Mind if I speak up?"

"Go ahead, Potter! Go ahead! Y'all can speak frankly at my table." Jim's grin was expansive. "Every man's got a right to his opinion."

"Well, maybe they don't make money," the man named Potter said, "but I was on that ride yesterday, and I saw them. They are beautiful to look at. And they're different. A domestic horse just doesn't have the same proud bearing. That wildness alone seems worth saving."

There was a murmur of agreement from the dozen-odd guests.

"Well put." Walker nodded at the man, then swung to face Jim. "They're part of our Western heritage."

"What a crock!" Jim barked. "Now, Potter, I hope you don't mind if I speak frankly to you." He studied the man from beneath beetled gray brows.

"Please." Potter sat straighter in his chair, obviously honored to have the ranch owner's full attention, something Stacey had noticed many of the guests vied for.

"You remind me of the wrangler here." Jim indicated Walker with a flourish of his butter knife. He proceeded to swipe a great glob of butter over a hunk of French bread, and Stacey wondered fleetingly why he called Walker "the wrangler" instead of his son, or even stepson. Did he want to avoid acknowledging their relationship?

"Like you, he goes all dewy-eyed over those rag tails," Jim went on. "Truthfully, I can't see it. They're scarred up from fighting—their heads are too big—they're ugly! One of these days, I'm gonna just give 'em all up to the BLM."

During his speech, Stacey noticed Walker's deepening frown. He held his fork in one brown fist. "And where will they put them? The BLM is doing as good a job as they can—I'll allow that—but it won't hurt us to protect those few small bands running in the hills." Walker was getting steamed up, Stacey could plainly see. But she also noted his strict control of himself; he was keeping his voice low and reasonable. "I've heard stories of slaughterhouses covertly adopting hundreds of them and quietly turning them into dog food."

Stacey uttered a soft gasp and heard others do the same.

"Now, boy, you know as well as I that there're laws against that. It's not supposed to happen anymore. But there's too many, anyhow. And this ranch isn't a federal reserve. It's private. When are you gonna realize those horses are a nuisance—eating up valuable forage, breaking down fences, trampling crops, dirtying up water holes. They're damaging the land for cattle!"

"No." Walker shook his head. "They spread grass seed and fertilize soil. Last winter when we had that snow that froze to ice, they broke trails for other animals and dug open iced-over water holes for the very cattle you're bellyaching about!"

Stacey could see Jim gearing up for a new argument. She lunged down the table for a bowl of vegetables. "More broccoli, Jim? I especially like the cheese sauce. Don't you?"

Both men looked at her in amazement. She could clearly read their thoughts—how dare she, an interfering female, break up a perfectly rousing argument? She felt her cheeks flush with chagrin, but determinedly thrust the bowl beneath the big man's chin. "Have some. You don't want Miriam to think you don't like it, do you?"

She needn't have made the attempt. Walker stood, dropping his cloth napkin on his chair. "You'll excuse me." He made it a statement. "I've got to check on that new foal." He nodded at Potter, then at Stacey, giving her a lingering glance she was at a loss to interpret. With that, he strode away.

If Jim thought Walker's exit was abrupt, he didn't show it. He merely waved the younger man off and continued to eat. The guests resumed their good-natured debate on wild horses versus stockmen, but Stacey's interest soon waned. Walker had been quite passionate in his defense of the creatures, and she'd found herself fascinated. When she'd first spotted him in the dining room, she'd felt wary; now she was sorry he'd left. He'd been adamant and opinionated. He'd been interesting.

After dinner, when Geoff suggested they go down to the barn to see the new foal, she agreed promptly, not because she wanted to see Walker, she told herself, but because she'd never seen a baby horse before. Walker was a hard, cold man. She'd had enough of that sort to last a lifetime.

The evening was chilly, and she wrapped an arm around Geoff's thin shoulders, shivering. He hugged her in return as they walked the short distance to the big barn. There were other children about, guests' kids, and a few ranch hands close to Geoff's age. Stacey hoped he'd get over his shyness soon and make friends with some of them.

Inside, old electric lanterns softly illuminated the haystack, its sweet smell permeating the air. Warmth from the bodies of the animals raised the temperature several degrees, making it a bit more comfortable.

From the other end of the barn she heard muted sounds of horse movements. At the bank of stalls Stacey peeked over each door until she found Walker, kneeling in the straw beside a bay-colored colt whose spindly legs were folded beneath its body. Next to him the colt's mother, a placid mare, chewed hay.

"Oh," Stacey breathed, "she's beautiful."

"It's a he," Walker corrected, stroking the foal's neck. "A colt. A female is a filly."

Geoff struggled to look over the top of the stall door, but he wasn't tall enough. "Can I see?"

"If you move slowly and talk in a quiet voice, you can come in," Walker said. "We don't want to upset the mama or frighten the colt." He again wore his brown hat, Stacey noticed, and although the night was cool, like her he hadn't put on a jacket.

Stacey unlatched the door, and Geoff slipped by. He knelt beside the colt and reached out a hand, touching the soft, fuzzy mane, his face reflecting his awe. Walker grinned at the child's expression and glanced at Stacey.

She caught her breath, struck anew by how very handsome he was when he smiled. His teeth were stark white against his skin, his dark-lashed eyes crinkling at the corners. The perpetual scowl had disappeared, and even the small bump on his nose seemed less apparent. Stacey found herself helpless to keep from smiling back shyly.

While Stacey watched, Geoff spent the next ten minutes bombarding the wrangler with myriad questions about the baby horse. Walker answered everything, explaining that this was a quarter horse, and that the breed had proven perfect for cattle work because of its strong shoulders and powerful hindquarters. "A quarter horse is able to make quick starts and tight turns," Walker explained. "And he's fast. The fastest in the world at the quarter mile."

"Wow." Geoff gently scratched between the colt's ears, as Walker showed him. "I really like horses."

"Yeah? What else do you like to do? Baseball?"

Geoff hesitated. "No."

"Then what? Soccer? Football?"

"Well . . ." The boy bit his lip, and Stacey bit hers, watching. "I read a lot. Especially about cowboys."

When Walker glanced at Stacey, there was a question in his eyes, and she felt the familiar seeping of despair.

"Reading's good," Walker allowed. "But don't you want to get outside, kick a ball around?"

Geoff shook his head.

"How about—" Walker began.

"Video games," Stacey put in quickly.

The boy's eyes brightened. "Yeah, I like video games."

"That's fine." Walker looked relieved. "Do you go to the arcades where all the kids hang around?"

Geoff blinked. "N-no. I mean the kind of game you hold in your hand. And . . . and I watch TV," he added.

Nodding slowly, Walker got to his feet and brushed the straw off his jeans. He led the boy out of the stall and closed the door. "I see. You like reading and hand-held games and television."

All the things you can do by yourself. Stacey knew what Walker implied. But her son had grown even more introverted since Dennis's death. Her heart wrenched. She'd tried getting him involved in sports; she'd tried encouraging him to play with others, but Geoff had simply withdrawn. No child psychologist, she had been at a loss to help him.

A month or so ago, one of her friends had kindly suggested that perhaps Geoff should see a counselor. Now Stacey wondered if she ought to seriously consider that option.

"Mom, I have to go to the bathroom."

Smiling through her worry, Stacey said, "Okay, run up to the house. It's almost time for bed."

"Aw, Mom." Geoff reluctantly got up and headed out the barn door.

Stacey drew a breath and faced Walker. "I've been a bit concerned about Geoff's unwillingness to participate in group sports or play with others. I admit that. But he's still recovering from his father's death. That hits a child hard. Even when—" She caught herself in horror. She'd been about to say "Even when the father is cold and uninvolved with his child." Clearing her throat, she struggled for poise and continued. "I don't want Geoff pressured."

Beneath his hat Walker's eyes were solemn, his voice soft. "Was I pressuring him?"

Turning a shoulder away, she studied her polished fingernails. "No. Not exactly."

"Well, I know how he feels. I lost my father when I was six. And my mother died when I was twelve."

Stacey whirled. How could she have been so insensitive? She put her hand on his arm. "Of course you know. I forgot." Beneath her fingers his forearm was warm, the muscles hard. "I'm sorry."

He shrugged, but his shadowed gaze never left her face. "It was tough. But I handled it."

"Yes," she said slowly, studying his features in return. "I imagine you did." Walker was strong, she knew that much, even if she still didn't know him very well. And at dinner, while he'd defended the wild horses, she'd seen in him a se-

rious concern for the environment and for wildlife. It drew
her to him, this caring.

"At dinner," she began, letting her hand slide away from
his arm, "I was impressed by your attitude. About the
horses, I mean."

He shrugged, taking three steps to collect a pair of half-
finished reins and begin braiding the leather. He looked up.
"I'm right, you know. The wild horses should be protected. Thirty years ago fewer than ten thousand were left."

Stacey felt her eyes widen. "That doesn't sound like
many."

"It's not." His mouth twisted. "Selfish ranchers across
the West, who wanted their leased land kept only for cattle,
used airplanes to roust them out of remote canyons and run
them off cliffs." Stacey gasped, but Walker went on grimly.
"Some went out with rifles and just picked them off, still
others poisoned water holes. Which, incidentally, killed
anything else drinking from them."

"My Lord," Stacey said sadly. "I'd no idea."

"Most people don't. But if it had been the elephant or
hippo, you can bet all this country's environmentalists
would've been up in arms." His tone was bitter, his words
clipped.

Stacey rubbed her arms. "What's going to happen to
them now?"

He studied her with cynical eyes. "You really want to
know?" At her nod, he shrugged. "About twenty years
back the Wild Horse Annie Act was pushed through. It
forbids capturing, branding or killing these horses, and it's
helped. The last estimate I read stated there are fifty or sixty
thousand now, although many of those have been adopted
and tamed by good, responsible people."

"I don't know much about horses," Stacey said. "But I
did see those yesterday. And I think they are beautiful."

"Yes. And the point is, they don't seriously damage the environment—no more than cows. I'd say so if they did. I'm a cattleman, too."

For several moments there was quiet between them while Stacey considered what Walker had told her. She rubbed her arms again, shivering a little. It was getting colder in the barn, but she had no wish to leave. Walker was not an ordinary cowboy, she could see that.

He half sat on a bale of hay that was placed outside the stall, one leg braced against the floor. She couldn't help noticing his long legs were lean but powerful, their outlines clear through his worn jeans.

After a moment he began talking again, almost to himself. "They're so proud and free looking. I want to protect them, yet sometimes even I feel the urge to go out and capture that freedom—tame it for my own." He put down the reins and met her gaze levelly. "But I overcome the urge. Too many have been caught by people like Jim and stripped of their dignity. If we take them all, we'll have lost the beauty and the wildness, and the world will have lost something precious. Lost it forever."

Stacey smiled tremulously. "You're very...eloquent."

His gaze slid away, and she could have sworn he ducked his head boyishly, as if she'd embarrassed him. It seemed as though cowboys used their hats for more than one purpose.

But then he rose from the bale and came toward her. When he was no more than twelve inches away, he said, "No one's ever called me eloquent before."

"Well." Her hands fluttered nervously. "You know what I mean."

"You were...complimenting me?" He came closer still, and Stacey found her breathing suddenly shallow. She backed up as unobtrusively as possible, but found the stall door barred further retreat. The rough wood met her shoulder blades.

"Yes," she told him. "It was a compliment. I'm sure most cowboys don't feel as passionately as you about wild-life."

He chuckled, the sound a deep rumble in his chest. "You know so many cowboys?"

"No. Actually . . . you're among the first." Even she had to chuckle as she said it.

They laughed together, and when the sounds died away, Walker flattened his palm on the doorjamb beside her head. Although there was nothing truly threatening about his manner, she still felt trapped. Deliciously so, and that worried her far more than anything he could do. "Truth is," Walker told her in a near whisper, "I can feel passionately about other things, as well."

"Really? How interesting." Stacey's eyes widened as Walker moved so close that he filled her field of vision entirely, and her nervousness grew. She ought to get out of here, go up to the house, go to bed safely, alone. But somehow Walker's compelling gaze mesmerized her.

She hardly knew this man, and what she did know, besides his concern for the wild horses, was not promising. Mostly he'd treated her rudely, his manner abrupt. But tonight he'd been polite, had answered all of her son's questions with admirable patience. He'd spoken to her as an equal, helped her to learn. He'd been respectful tonight, at least, and now she found her carefully built defenses weakening. She ought to move.

"Why'd you come out here tonight, Stacey?" he wondered in that same low voice.

"I—to see the baby horse."

"Uh-huh. That all?"

"Of course. What else would there be?"

"Yeah. What else?"

The barn went dead silent. No hinges creaked in the old wooden doors, no horse blew or stamped, no wind whistled through the rafters. There was only Walker, close enough to kiss her.

The quiet undid her.

She stepped aside, away from the cage of his arm. Searching her mind for a safe topic, she blurted, "About Geoff... I'm thinking of taking him to see a child psychologist. Maybe the two of us need counseling. So when we get back home—"

Walker snorted, dropping his arm. "That's a *city* solution." He said the word contemptuously. "It's just what a modern woman like you would do—let somebody else take care of your problems. That kid doesn't need anyone messing with his mind. He just needs attention."

Stung, Stacey faced him again, her arms crossed defensively. If he'd thrown a bucket of frigid water over her, he couldn't have doused the mood faster. With just a few cutting words he'd made her feel stupid, and an inadequate parent, as well. She struck back. "Attention? Well, it won't be from you."

"Hell, no! Not me. I'm no surrogate daddy."

She lifted her chin. "Fine. We understand each other then. Good night." With that she walked stiffly toward the door, making as dignified an exit as she could. Behind her the door banged, but it didn't make her feel any better.

Walker swore softly, cursing himself for a fool. In the instant Stacey's chin had come up so proudly, he'd realized that he'd insulted her motherhood. He should never have thrown out that "surrogate daddy" line.

Jamming the half-finished reins onto their hook, he turned out the lights and closed up the barn. Well, he never had learned how to handle women. Some men had a way with them. They knew what to say and when, but he'd never had the knack, and before now, he hadn't truly cared. He hadn't meant to be so brusque, but he guessed that over the years surliness had become second nature.

Walker was a sardonic, bitter man, and he knew it.

Passing through the outer corral that led to the house, he barely noticed the chill breeze that flattened the shirt against his chest. He was tough, and the elements rarely bothered him. Growing up here and expected to perform a man's work by the time he was thirteen hadn't been easy, but he'd done it. And he'd done it under Jim's harsh hand. He guessed that hand had shaped him more than he cared to think.

Had Stacey wanted him to kiss her, as she'd seemed to? Her signals had appeared clear, even to a relatively inexperienced man like himself. If he'd misread her and blown his chance he'd...

At the outer gate he paused, catching the shadowy reflection of his face in the still water of the trough. His customary scowl was in place, and even at night, with a half moon overhead, he could discern the ugly bump marring his nose.

No. He'd made no mistake. Desirable women like Stacey had never wanted him before, so why would one now? He'd been fooling himself. The conclusion was bitter but logical, and he knew he must accept the truth.

Inside, Stacey was surprised to find that all the other guests had retired for the night; most of them must have been exhausted by the day of unaccustomed riding and fresh air, she thought. Just as she paused in the living room in front of the roaring fire, Jim lumbered in from the kitchen and spotted her staring into the flames.

"Here, girl, what's wrong?" He put his huge, pawlike hand on her shoulder and looked into her eyes, his bushy gray brows lowered.

"Nothing. Nothing's wrong, Jim. It's just...Walker and I—"

"Walker! That boy upsetting you?"

"Jim, I'm not upset. But he feels I want to—to somehow take over his place here." She folded her hands in front of her.

"That's crazy. If you'd been after this place, you'da' tried for it long before now. Damn that Walker for upsettin' you! I'll just tie that boy in a knot."

Walker stepped through the front door. He squared off toward Jim, tense, stiff. "You're welcome to try."

Jim rounded on his stepson, ignoring his comment. "What's in your mind, arguing with Stacey and her only here two days?"

"Jim." Stacey stepped between them, not about to let this get out of hand. "I wasn't so nice, either. It wasn't his fault."

Putting his big hands upon his hips, Jim glared at them both. His voice, normally booming, rose to a thunder. "Now are you telling me you two don't get along? It ain't right—the two of you arguing. Why, you're practically brother and sister."

Stacey, unused to having his wrath directed at her, felt herself wilting. She cringed guiltily. She hadn't thought much about her familial relationship to Walker, but she *had* been married to his stepbrother, the boy he'd grown up with.

Walker said nothing at all. She wondered if he felt bad about his harsh words.

"Furthermore," Jim went on, still glowering at Walker, "I won't allow you to run Stacey off like you did Dennis some twelve years ago!"

At that Walker turned white. Stacey, sensing his shock, tried hard to assimilate her own. Dennis had never said anything about being "run off" his family ranch. The only time he'd ever mentioned it had been to say he hated ranch life and would never go back.

Beneath his breath Walker spat something that sounded like a curse, turned on his heel and stalked out. Stacey watched him go, bewildered by the antagonism that had arced between the two men. She turned back to Jim.

"I wanted to wait awhile longer," Jim said in a tired voice. "To give you time to get to like the place. But now I

see the time is right. We'd best talk." He held out a hand,
indicating the doorway opposite that led into his office.

Even more bewildered, Stacey walked into the room on
numb feet. When Jim sat down heavily behind the enormous desk, she perched on the edge of a small chair before
it. Her hands were cold, so she chafed them together. For
some reason she felt like a small child who'd been called into
the principal's office for punishment. It was silly! She was
a grown woman, for goodness sake.

Jim swiveled his chair toward a short filing cabinet,
withdrawing a sheaf of papers, which he laid on the desk,
facing her. Then he sat back, threading his fingers together
and resting his linked hands across his ample girth.

With an odd feeling of apprehension, Stacey lifted the top
sheet and read it, then scanned the second and the third.
When she finished, she sat back in her own chair, gaping at
Jim.

"This is your will," she stated, her voice squeaky.

"A living trust, to be precise," he corrected. "And as you
can see, when I die, my fifty-percent ownership in this ranch
will be inherited by your son, Geoff. You will be the execu-
tor."

Chapter Four

Her fingers at her throat, Stacey gasped. "You're leaving all this—" she spread her arms "—to . . . to Geoff?"

"And to you. If I . . . er, saddle a cloud and ride into the Great Beyond before the boy is twenty-one, you'll run the show. You and Walker, that is."

"Oh, yes," Stacey said in a small voice. "Walker. What does he think about this?"

Something about the way Jim lifted one massive shoulder tipped her off. She looked at him closely. "He doesn't know, does he?"

"Didn't see any need to tell him." Jim's belligerence returned. "What's the difference? I can do what I want with my half of this place." He leaned across the desk and his manner suddenly changed. Grinning, he told her, "Meantime, I aim to live a spell longer. Till I'm gone, I want you and the boy here."

"But what will Walker say when he hears?"

"Will you quit worrying that bone?" Jim gathered the papers into a pile and jammed them back into the filing cabinet. "What Walker thinks don't signify. He's got no say in the matter. Now you and the boy will move here permanently. You can go to town and collect what you've left behind. Geoff'll have a good life living on this ranch. And when he's older, I'll pay for any college he likes."

"Yes, Jim," Stacey replied dutifully, but her mind was awhirl with the possibilities. She was worried about Walker's reaction, but overwhelming her were the positive ramifications of the will. Geoff would own property! A thrilling future awaited her son. He would live in this place he appeared to love. He would have a good college education— something she had no hope of providing for him. And she would have a permanent home! Roots!

She was surprised when Jim launched into a tirade. "I've worked twenty years to build myself a good reputation in these mountains. I've helped the neighbors, agreed to let the Indians use the water, served on local committees. I've busted my butt to show everyone that Jim Maloney's a square shooter. I'm proud of my reputation, girl. So don't talk to me about Walker."

"Jim. I—I don't know what to say. I'm...thank you."

The big man made a show of sifting through other files. He waved a hand carelessly. "Don't mention it. Want that grandson around, that's all. And I guess you're okay, too, for a female."

Stacey smiled. She got up, moved around the desk and planted a big kiss on the startled man's cheek. "You come across like a grizzly bear, but you're not so tough, after all."

"Here now, leave off." He pushed her away. "I've got things to do."

"Yes, Jim," she said again, heading out of the office. She didn't want to think about Walker's reaction. Maybe he wouldn't be so terribly upset.

He was the first person she ran into.

He grasped her by the elbows before she could barrel into him. "What are you so happy about?"

Instantly her smile vanished. She backed away and darted a guilty glance toward the shadowy door of Jim's office. Walker followed her eyes, then pinned her again with a searching stare. "Well?"

"Maybe you'd best talk to Jim," Stacey evaded, having no wish to bring Walker the news. She admitted that there was a bit of a coward in her. A tiny bit. "In fact, he's in his office right now. Why don't you—"

"Why don't *you* tell me?"

The coward in Stacey blossomed. "I've got to make sure Geoff is tucked in—and I'm very tired. I'll just go on to bed."

"The hell you will." Walker shot out a hand and clamped her wrist. "I want to know right now. What's going on?"

He wasn't really hurting her, but his long, sun-browned fingers wrapped around her slim wrist were very firm. She squirmed, trying to get loose. "It's just...it's a few plans Jim has made, that's all. He can explain them ever so much better than I—"

"Now, Stacey."

"It's his will." She drew a deep breath and stopped trying to get free. "He's leaving his share of the ranch to Geoff."

Beneath the dark shelf of his lowered brows, Walker's green eyes blazed and his pupils dilated. His mouth twisted cynically, and with an abruptness that startled her, he let go of her wrist. "No wonder you're so happy. What a surprise. I guess you got what you came for, huh? Satisfied?"

"No. No—I didn't. I told you I wasn't...." Her voice faded weakly; it was obvious Walker didn't believe her, and nothing she could say would change that. She drew herself up. "Listen, I know this was your mother's property before she married Jim, and I respect that. You feel entitled to it. But it's apparent to me that Jim worked for his share." Since he didn't interrupt, she continued, picking up steam. "And I don't want to steal anything from you, Walker. But maybe I can help here. Maybe I can make suggestions for better efficiency. Yes, that's an idea." She stepped forward and in her enthusiasm, touched his sleeve. "I noticed while I was in Jim's office that the bookkeeping seems a little slapdash. Perhaps I could improve—"

"I'm afraid I don't like your language." Walker almost spat out the words.

"What?"

He shook off her hand. "Your words. *Improve. Change. New ideas.*" His hard gaze raked her up and down. "What do you know about cattle ranching? What do you know about running a guest facility?"

"Not a lot, but I can learn."

"You'll only get in the way, be a pest. Interfere where you're not needed or wanted. First off, you'll probably want to redecorate." He shook his head as if she'd already torn down the old drapes. Hands on hips, he paused a moment, delivering his next line with chilling derision. "Who needs you?"

Swallowing hard, Stacey faced him in silence. She hated his aggressive manner, hated his unfounded accusations and his preconceived notions of womanhood. She wanted to shout at him that he was wrong, wrong, wrong!

But she couldn't tell him that; a knot in her throat threatened to choke her. Tears, she knew, would spell weakness to a man like Walker. They'd only reinforce his idea of her as an emotional female.

She would not cry.

Walker stood before her, his fury nearly swamping him. At the same time he felt a crazy, unbidden leap of excitement. As always, when he stood close to her, he felt the sharp edge of sexual awareness. Beautiful, desirable Stacey would be a permanent part of his life now, in some way or other. The conflicting mix of emotions only served to stoke his anger. He didn't want to feel this way! He wanted to hate her.

Muttering an epithet, he whirled away from the hurt vulnerability he saw in her big eyes. She had no right to look like that—this was *his* ranch, not some meddling female's!

Stomping past her, he went to his bedroom at the end of the long hall and closed the door. It was dark, with only the moon's thin light creeping in through the open drapes. Sitting on his bed, he yanked off one boot, then the other, letting them fall to the hardwood floor with loud thunks. He threw his hat toward the rack by the door, and as usual, missed. The brown Stetson hit the wall, bounced off and rolled around the floor on its brim.

Walker swore beneath his breath. He didn't for a second consider trying to talk to Jim. The big man made his decisions and stuck by them. As long as Walker had known him, he'd never been dissuaded from anything. The man was as hardheaded as a mule. But he'd never given Walker cause to believe that the ranch would belong to anyone other than Walker himself. Walker had always assumed that when the time came, the Bar M would be solely his to run, his to own completely.

But now Jim had unearthed a grandson, of all things. Another owner would complicate Walker's life forever.

He was a fighting man, one who didn't know the meaning of the word "surrender." And he planned to keep on fighting, but for a moment futility overwhelmed him.

He sat on his bed with its old, faded quilt and scarred wooden headboard. Just sat there, elbows on knees, looking at his dusty hat. He was alone, as he'd always been, and probably always would be. No woman would ever have him, not with his looks. And even he knew his temperament was about as warm as a crowbar on a January morning. Who would want him? A lonely cowboy, struggling with all his might to hang on to the one thing in the world that mattered to him: his land.

Rising wearily, he walked to the simple pine chest that held his clothes and squatted to open the bottom drawer.

Deep in the back, under a stack of sweaters he never wore, his hand touched the edges of an envelope, which was brittle and faded brown from age. Extracting it, he stood and flicked the switch of a small lamp that rested on top of his chest of drawers.

The dim light shone weakly upon the unmarked envelope in his fist. For a moment he simply stared at it, thinking. Then, slowly, he removed a photograph. A twenty-year-old photograph. In it, a much-younger Jim was shown working. But the work he was performing clearly was not legal.

It was a deep, shameful secret Jim had hid. But Walker knew. He had this photograph. And his memories. Someday, Walker swore, he might produce his evidence to the world, and in this way he'd get what he wanted. Yes, someday he might just do it.

Walker reluctantly put the photo back into the envelope and shoved it beneath the sweaters.

Five a.m. came far too quickly on this ranch, Stacey decided, waking when Geoff bounced on her bed. Since she'd never had to get up before seven for her nine a.m. city job, she'd rarely seen dawn. She eyed him balefully from her snug nest of blankets. "Geoff, this is not my idea of a fun way to wake up."

Her son grinned. "Aw, Mom, come on. It's already five o'clock! We can go down and help get the horses ready!"

"Whoopee," she said dryly. "Every morning this week you've bounced on my bed, and every morning I've told you I don't want to get the horses ready. Honestly, Geoff, when are you going to learn?"

"But I want to, Mom."

"Then go on."

"Thanks!" He bounded out before the last word had escaped her mouth. Despite her sleepiness, she grinned. In the short week they had been on the ranch Geoff had already acquired a light tan, which in itself was encouraging, considering his pallor over the past year. And he was eager to get up each day, thrilled to work with the animals and whatever friendly wrangler happened to be around. It was just ironic it was usually Walker.

Stacey sat up in bed and brushed tangled hair out of her face. It was fortunate that although Walker treated her with cool cynicism, he did not extend his negative feelings to the boy. At least he was mature enough not to make an innocent ten-year-old pay for adults' actions.

On the contrary, whenever she spotted Geoff tagging along at Walker's heels, the two of them appeared to get along well. On one occasion she'd seen Walker patiently demonstrate to Geoff how to tie a cinch knot. Another day she saw Walker hand Geoff a new pair of chaps, scaled to fit his small body. "For me?" Geoff had inquired, and when the wrangler nodded, the boy was obviously pleased. Walker gave a no-big-deal shrug and pulled on his own chaps.

Although Walker had taken the guests out each day to see if they could spot the wild horses again, the horses had stayed out of sight.

But when the group returned late that afternoon, Geoff flew off his horse, rushing up to Stacey. She was perched atop the wooden rails of the corral, enjoying the sunshine, where she usually waited for Geoff. Breathless, he told her, "Mom, we finally saw them! They've moved to a new pasture a little higher up—Walker says probably to get the greener grass there since summer's half over."

"How nice, Geoff," Stacey replied, smiling. The other riders trailed into the corral, followed by Walker. As usual, his expression was shadowed by his hat, but he gave her a hard, appraising glance that told her he was aware of her.

The guests dismounted and one of them, a good-natured man who liked Geoff, said, "The boy spotted them first." Stacey recognized him as Potter, the man who'd argued politely with Jim over the wild horses. She noticed he still wore the purple bandanna around his neck. "And because he found them for us, the wrangler allowed him to name that big sorrel stallion."

"Yeah." Geoff stuck out his thin chest, swelling with pride.

Stacey flicked a quick glance at Walker, who was silently tying the horses to the corral fence. He ignored her.

"Well?" She turned to Geoff. "Don't keep me in suspense. What did you name him?"

Thrusting his hands deep into the front pockets of his jeans, the boy rocked back on his heels and frowned in concentration, looking for all the world like a grizzled old cowman preparing to tell a good yarn. Stacey fought back a smile.

"You see," Geoff began, "there he was, standing on top of a long ridge. But his back was to the west—I remember, because they told us in school the sun sets in the west. Anyway, behind him the sun was going down, and it kind of...of sparked, like flames around him. You know, he's got that red coat that's so pretty?" Stacey nodded. "So I thought we'd call him Ridgefire. Do you like it?"

She ruffled his hair. "Yes, son. It's a real good name."

He nodded importantly. "Walker said so. He said the name would stick."

Without looking up from where he stood, Walker nodded. Stacey could see that although he wanted to ignore her, he was listening to every word. She said to her son, "Did you thank Walker for that honor?"

Geoff approached him at a quick trot. "Thanks, Wild Horse Walker."

Stacey noticed he couldn't hide his smile. He tousled the boy's hair, just as she had done. "Don't mention it."

Back at Stacey's side, Geoff threw his arms around her waist in sheer exuberance. "Gosh, Mom, this place is radical! I wish we could live here forever and ever!"

Surprised into silence, Stacey hugged him back. She had deliberately told Geoff nothing about Jim's will, not wanting to excite him if anything changed. Perhaps Jim hadn't meant to make it sound as though moving there was a prerequisite to inheriting the ranch. But it had.

Racing off, Geoff followed Potter and the other guests back to the house to get his horse an apple. Stacey lingered in the corral, alone with Walker. The air was still and warm, a little dust lending it an earthy smell. Evening was approaching; darkness came swiftly when the sun disappeared behind the mountains. Stacey said, "Um, I know you don't like me much, but I want you to know I'm grateful that you're being kind to Geoff. That was a nice thing you did, allowing him to feel important by naming that horse."

For the first time Walker let his gaze meet hers. "I haven't done anything for Geoff I wouldn't for any other kid who came to stay on this ranch."

Stacey nodded solemnly, and Walker went back to work. But she wondered if that was true. Somehow she didn't think Walker was quite as indifferent as he would have her believe.

"So you see, I do have concerns about what will happen." Stacey took the same chair in Jim's office two days later. She nervously sat on the edge. In the past few days thoughts of what she ought to do had consumed her. She wanted her son happy, wanted him to have all he deserved but she also had to consider herself, however selfish it seemed.

"What's the problem?" Jim's bushy brows rose as he lounged back in his chair behind the desk.

"Don't you understand, Jim? You're asking me to leave all I know. Leave my home of over ten years. It'll be hard to leave my friends, people Dennis and I knew socially—played tennis with. What about where I—I shop? Get my hair cut?

Have my car repaired? A person gets used to going to the same places, you know.''

She met his gaze and knew she sounded silly. She'd find new places to do all those things here in the mountains. But her feelings weren't entirely rational. They were emotional.

He merely looked at her.

She gave it one last stab. "Even my mother lives in Los Angeles.''

"Bring your mother up here. She'd love ranch life." Jim waved a careless hand.

"No." Stacey shook her head ruefully. "She's newly married to a nice man I like very much, but they're definitely city people. You know, Jim, this could be tough on Geoff. He'd have to change schools, make new friends, too.''

"The boy'll love it. So will you. Just give it time. In a coupla' years, you won't believe you ever lived in the city. Don't worry about a thing.''

Stacey was hard put to it not to roll her eyes. He made it all seem so incredibly easy. Yet she knew it would not be so. There were roadblocks here, Walker chief among them. He did his best to show her he wanted no part of her. Stacey sighed, rising. She had more thinking to do.

At dinner, Walker didn't speak to her at all, freezing her out. And when she went to bed that night, she stretched her legs beneath the covers, imagining the kind of man she wanted in her life now. Walker was curt and antagonistic, diametrically opposed to her ideal.

No, she wanted a good-natured sort. Someone happy in his world and pleased to share life with her. A demonstrative mate, someone who would tell her each day he loved her, perhaps offer her romantic gifts—maybe sachets or roses. One who'd like to touch her, she decided, run his hand down her cheek, gaze lovingly into her eyes.

Stacey rolled over and plumped her pillow, snuggling down again. She was attracted to a tall, tanned man who walked with confidence and easy athleticism. If he happened to wear a dark cowboy hat pulled low over his eyes, why, she didn't mind...

Startling herself, she caught her breath. Walker's face swam before her. Why couldn't she get the disagreeable man out of her mind? He had no reason to haunt her thoughts, far from it! On the surface she trusted him little, and half expected him to try and talk Jim into changing his will. And on a deeper, emotional level her trust was nonexistent. Walker was the sort of man to break an unwary woman's heart.

Oh, he was handsome enough, and in his arrogant swagger there was an undeniable sexuality she suspected most females would be hard put to overlook. She imagined many women would be drawn to the bad boy in him. The few times he'd touched her had been electric, and she had no doubt that in bed his lovemaking would send her up in flames.

She couldn't afford to get too near that fire.

On the tenth day Stacey decided to make herself useful. She offered to help Jim with the bookkeeping, which he politely, but flatly, refused. She offered to help the housekeepers clean rooms or change linens. They thanked her, saying no.

Frustrated and at loose ends, she wandered down to the corral just as a one-horse trailer, hauled by a pickup truck, pulled up. Walker greeted the driver and they both went around to the trailer, Geoff, as usual, dogging Walker's heels.

Stacey sat on the bottom porch step, watching. She could hear only snatches of their conversation.

The driver, a handsome teenage boy, backed a dapple-gray gelding down the trailer ramp. The teenager demonstrated the gentle nature of the horse, who led docilely about the packed-dirt yard.

"Okay, Dan," she heard Walker say as he accepted the lead rope, "Come on back in a few days, and we'll see what we can do."

The young man climbed into his truck and slammed the door. "Good luck," he said, and in his voice Stacey could hear a wry note. He sped off.

Instructing Geoff to sit on top of the rails, Walker led the horse into the front corral and proceeded to put a saddle onto its back. The second he tightened the cinch the horse threw a fit, jumping around, eyes rolling. Rearing up, it stood suspended in the air a few seconds, then fell over backward. Walker stepped neatly out of the way.

Stacey gasped, coming to her feet. She hurried to Geoff and stood beside where he sat, leaning her arms on the rails. The horse lay on the ground, making no attempt to get up. Walker merely nodded to himself, as if he'd expected this behavior all along.

"It's a bad habit," he explained to Geoff. "Nobody can ride a horse like this. We call them cinch binders. Dan tells me this horse won't get up for love nor money until the cinch is released." As if to prove it, he nudged the gray's belly with his booted toe. The horse did not react. Walker turned, surprising Stacey by acknowledging her. He touched his hat. "Afternoon."

"Good afternoon," she replied.

"Bucking's one thing. We can ride the buck out of a horse if necessary. Then he can be trained to carry a rider properly. This is something else again."

"Cinch binders," Geoff repeated seriously. "What are you going to do?"

The wrangler inclined his head. "We'll try something, see if we can't convince him to behave. This isn't a bad horse. Just a little too clever for his own good. He's figured a way to get out of work." Suddenly he grinned. "Something I haven't figured out yet."

Geoff giggled, and Stacey blinked. Walker's quicksilver moods kept her off balance. This time she wouldn't trust his current lightheartedness to last. This time she'd stay cautiously neutral.

"Can I help you, Walker?" Geoff asked. "I want to learn how to train the horse."

"You'll learn by watching this time. I want you both to stay up there where you're safe." Keeping out of the way of the sharp hooves, Walker released the cinch strap, and the gelding rolled to its feet. He kept a firm hold on the halter. "It's a dangerous habit for a horse to learn, this falling back. He could seriously hurt a rider, even kill somebody doing that. It's our job to teach him to quit."

Careful to tie the horse securely to a fence post, Walker took the saddle back to the tack room and came back with a leather strap, rigged with what appeared to be a handhold on top. "This is called a surcingle, or bull rigging. Usually it's used for riding bulls, but today we'll let Graybeard here try it."

"You're going to ride this horse?" Stacey asked, horrifying images of Walker crushed beneath the thousand-pound animal flashing before her.

"Nah. He's not ready to get ridden. Got to teach him some manners first." In his other hand he carried a length of woven nylon. Untying the horse, he let the lead rope trail on the ground, then quickly cinched the surcingle about the horse's belly. As before, the horse reacted violently, rearing up and falling back onto the hard-packed dirt.

This time Walker stepped forward, quickly circling the horse's legs with the nylon length until all four legs were bound together. He stood back with a satisfied expression. "There now, you old jughead. We'll see how you like that."

"Now what?" Stacey asked. This horse training was fascinating. And Walker had changed, at least temporarily. He'd become approachable, willing to share his thoughts, and Stacey found herself irresistibly drawn to him. She climbed up to sit beside Geoff.

"We'll let him think about it for an hour or so."

An hour did pass, during which Walker several times took his suede chaps and flapped them over the horse's body from head to tail. Graybeard tried to get up to no avail, not liking the chapping. A couple times Walker let out a few Indian war whoops close to the horse's ear for good measure. Again, Graybeard struggled, but he couldn't get free.

Walker smiled at Stacey and her son and suddenly it hit her—it was the horses! Walker didn't relate well to people. But with horses he was at his best. He knew how they thought, how they were going to behave, even before they did.

If only he could learn to be as happy around people. Stacey stared at him, thinking hard. He'd grown up with only Dennis and Jim, both hard, cold men. Walker had had no softness since his mother died. No one to help him find gentleness inside. Stacey was sure she'd seen it with the horses. And with Geoff.

The horse tried to get up now, even when Walker wasn't harrying him, but still couldn't make it.

"How long are you gonna make him lie there?" Geoff asked.

"Well…" Walker made a show of scratching his ear "…I don't rightly know. What's your opinion?"

Geoff frowned and pursed his lips with all the importance a ten-year-old can muster. "I think he's about ready."

"If you say so." Walker bent, untying the horse's legs and when the gelding got up, it licked its lips. "A sure sign he's ready to cooperate," he commented. The animal allowed itself to be led around the corral, then saddled. When the cinch was tightened, it grunted, but didn't lift its forelegs off the ground, even an inch.

Carefully Walker mounted, then went ahead and worked the horse in the corral, jogging, trotting and finally cantering in circles. "This horse is broke," he announced at last, getting down. "I don't think he'll try his old trick anymore."

The gray nuzzled Walker's arm, sniffed his ear and raised its lips to Walker's, almost as if it wanted to kiss the man. Stacey gaped. It was crazy—even she knew horses didn't kiss! But the transformation in the animal was amazing. Walker truly had a magic touch.

Stacey smiled to herself, trying to figure how to go about teaching Walker to find gentleness in himself. He wasn't mean, just hard. It was an ingrained habit, anyone could see it.

But if she was clever, she might be able to get him to laugh, to enjoy life more, make him easier to deal with, without him ever knowing it was happening.

Walker pulled off the saddle, gave the gray a quick rubdown and turned him into an adjacent corral with the other horses. Geoff jumped off the rails, racing into the barn to play with the goats, and Walker strolled toward Stacey. He let out a long, satisfied breath and leaned back on the rail a few feet away, hooking one boot on the lowest rung.

"Good work, Walker," Stacey said. She smiled softly at him.

Her approval made him feel good. Real good. "Thanks," he mumbled.

"You dealt effectively with Graybeard. But you were never cruel to him."

"Naw. Cruelty isn't necessary when you work with horses. You just have to understand the way they think."

"And you do." She made it a definite statement.

"I s'pose." He glanced at her from under his hat and found her still smiling at him, her blue eyes wide and admiring. Quickly he looked away, but within seconds he found himself drawn back, meeting her gaze again. Her admiration was a powerful lure, he found, and her whole demeanor was inviting. Even the way she sat on the fence, sort of tilted toward him, almost . . . eager.

His body's reaction at the thought was predictable, he figured, shifting uncomfortably. And he wasn't surprised. From the first moment he'd laid eyes on the woman, he'd wanted her. And even learning what really lay behind her visit to the Bar M hadn't doused the growing heat he'd felt for her.

She could seduce him with very little effort, he realized, not that he expected she'd try. He didn't trust her about the ranch, but somehow he knew Stacey would never use her body to get her way. There was a primness about her, a sexy innocence that should be out of place in a woman thirty years old and the mother of a ten-year-old, to boot. But it wasn't.

It was just the way she was.

A breath of her delicate violet fragrance wafted toward him. He inhaled, liking her scent more than he should. "Perfume?" he asked, figuring it was a safe enough question.

"What? Oh, no. I never wear it. I guess you're smelling my bath soap."

A vision of a damp, deliciously nude Stacey, rising slowly from her bath, skin dewy and sweet from her violet soap, materialized in Walker's mind. He swallowed hard, thinking how her plump breasts would look, how she'd hold out her hand, welcoming him into the water.

"Walker, I wish I was as skilled at something as you are. I can do some things pretty well, but I'm not an expert at anything."

He chuckled. She was extremely skilled at getting him hard and hot and needing her; she just didn't know it.

"What's so funny?" Climbing down, she stood before him.

"Nothing."

"Listen." she touched his chest, and he realized she touched him a lot. He wondered if she was aware of it. "We're able to talk if we try, aren't we? I think you and I can get along well. What do you say?"

For a long moment he studied her, staring into her open face and fighting the urge to pull her against his hard frame and kiss her shoes off.

Suspicion intervened.

Perhaps, just perhaps, she *did* know the power she held over him. Maybe she wasn't too pure to use it, either. It wouldn't be the first time a woman manipulated a man for her own ends. If he succumbed to her, he could well be falling into a trap as old as the world itself.

Straightening, he covered her hand with his own and put it aside with a deliberate movement. "You're laying it on a little thick, aren't you, darlin'? I wasn't born yesterday, you know."

Her brow wrinkled. "I don't understand."

"I'm immune to your feminine wiles. And I won't be manipulated. Got it?"

She looked at him with wounded eyes. "Is that what you think?"

He nodded once. "It surely is."

The corners of her pretty mouth firmed, and he forced himself to look away. It wouldn't do him any good to relax his guard against her now.

She was talking in earnest tones. "Evidently Jim planned to leave Geoff his portion of this place before we even got here. The living trust was all made out by his attorney. Even you must know that. What have I to gain by manipulating you?"

He shrugged, still cynical. "If you can control me, you've got the reins of this ranch."

"That's crazy. Nobody's got that much influence over anyone. And like you said, I don't know anything about running a business like this." She reached out to touch him

again, then withdrew her hand, as if reconsidering.
"Walker, please, I'm telling the truth. Can't we start over,
get along?"

"We'll get along all right," he told her, brushing by to
head up to the house. "Just stay out of my way."

Stacey watched him stalk off and felt some of her hope
drain away. It was going to be even tougher than she'd first
imagined, gentling this man. Much, much tougher.

Chapter Five

The rumble of a truck's engine woke Stacey the next morning. For once Geoff had sneaked out without bouncing on her bed. Wondering who would be going anywhere so early, she groggily got up on all fours and parted the curtains to peer out.

She recognized the gray, leonine head in the driver's seat and watched, rubbing her eyes, while Jim roared off with his usual abandon, clearly heading for town. The digital clock glowed six-thirty, not as early as she'd thought, but even with the hour-and-a-half drive ahead of him, it was still too early for any kind of shopping in Bakersfield. Few businesses opened before ten, or at least nine, and Jim would be down the mountain by eight a.m. It made no sense!

At that moment she decided to ask him outright where he went when he drove to town. She was sure he'd have a simple reason, and her curiosity would be assuaged. It wasn't that she was nosy; she was truly beginning to care about the big, gruff man. He'd offered her and her son so much, and asked nothing in return.

By noon Jim was back, the truck's tires spraying gravel and dust. Off on a trail ride, Walker had been gone for hours. Geoff was in the barn with a son of one of the ranch hands, performing who knew what chore. Stacey did not want to interrupt Geoff's first attempt at making a friend here. She was still worried about his inability to relate to children of his own age. The ranch hand's son, Scotty, was just a year older than Geoff, but a rough-and-tumble sort who'd grown up in the country. He must stand half a head taller and outweigh Geoff by a good fifteen pounds, she guessed. All the same, when the boy had been struggling with an electronic space-invaders game, Geoff had given him a few tips, and a tenuous friendship had been struck.

The two boys came out of the barn when they heard Jim's truck, Geoff leading the smallest, whitest horse Stacey had ever seen. "Oh," Stacey breathed, forgetting for a moment to ask Jim where he'd been. She climbed through the rails and put out a hand to stroke the tiny muzzle. "Geoff, you told me there was a miniature horse here, but I guess I'd forgotten. He's darling!"

Jim opened the gate, coming inside. "Yep, Snowball's cute, huh? We keep him for the kids who visit. They love him."

"I love him," Stacey said, measuring the top of its withers against her leg. "He couldn't be three feet tall!"

Geoff grinned, holding the halter's lead rope. "Scotty told me he's the smallest kind of horse in the world."

"He is little," Stacey agreed.

"Nobody can ride him," Scotty put in. "But he can pull a cart in harness. Sometimes I hitch him up for the little kids who're too young to go on trail rides. It's fun."

Geoff patted Snowball's neck. "I wish I could ride him. But I guess my feet would drag on the ground."

"We'll get you your own horse, son," Jim said. "Would you like that?"

The boy went still, his eyes widening. "*Would* I!"

"A boy on a ranch needs his own horse. It's a good way to learn responsibility, to care for an animal. Now let me see." He stroked his chin. "Not a Welsh pony or a Shetland. You need something you can grow with. Probably a small quarter horse. Something well trained. Gentle. I'll ask Walker what we've got."

"Jim," Stacey said warningly. "I haven't . . . uh, come to a decision yet."

"About what, Mom?" Geoff piped up, his gaze moving quickly from Jim to her.

"About living here?" Jim boomed. "I thought that was all settled."

"You mean you'll let us?" Geoff jumped up and down. "Can we stay here, Mom? Can we?"

She eyed Jim balefully. "We'll see, son."

"But, Mom, Grandpa said we could. And I can work with the horses every day and you can . . . you can watch me!" He said it as if this endeavor would fill the better part of her day. "And you don't have to go back to that old job of yours."

This was getting out of hand. "Geoff, that's enough. I said we'll see." Over his head, she directed what she hoped was a glower at Jim.

The big man was not intimidated. He took her arm, a sly grin splitting his face as he led her toward the house. "You going to disappoint that boy, missy?"

"That's not the issue." She tried to glare at him, but failed. Sighing, she knew she wasn't really angry with Jim; Geoff would have had to be told about the offer sooner or later, anyway. "I have to decide what's best. I just don't know yet."

He patted her hand, linked in his arm. "You'll make the right decision. I'm not worried about it."

Stacey gave up arguing, remembering her question for him. "I saw you leave this morning for Bakersfield. That is where you went, isn't it?"

The big man grunted.

"Is there . . . perhaps a woman you're seeing?" she asked tentatively.

"What? Nah, I gave up on women years ago. Too much trouble."

"I see. Have you joined some sort of club, then? Going to meetings?"

He shook his head.

"Shopping?"

They were at the house now. He opened the door and looked down at her stiffly. "Just town business."

"Ah." She nodded as if she understood, but, of course, she didn't. Why all the secrecy, she wondered, her curiosity deepening. Why so vague?

Inside, they gathered with the guests for lunch, and Miriam, the cook, pulled Jim aside. Since Stacey was still at his side, she could overhear the low exchange.

"I don't feel so good," Miriam was saying, a resting hand on her midriff. "I got lunch ready, but Rudy's taking over for dinner. He's not much of a cook, but I already did most of the work and told him when to put the casserole in."

Jim nodded. "You go on home, Miriam. Rest. It's probably just the flu. Been going around, you know. Rudy'll do just fine till tomorrow. We'll see you in the morning."

The plump woman nodded tiredly, pulling off her apron as she disappeared into the kitchen.

"Is she okay?" Stacey whispered, concerned by the older woman's pallor.

"Sure. She's salt of the earth. Take a lot to keep her down." Jim waved off her worry and in a louder voice urged everyone to sit. "She'll be back tomorrow, you'll see."

But she wasn't.

Stacey learned early the next morning that Miriam had been rushed down the mountain during the night for an emergency appendectomy. There were complications, and the surgery had been difficult. Miriam's recovery would take weeks longer than usual.

It took only seconds to make the decision. Stacey collected a frayed, red gingham apron and tied it on. "I'll take over," she announced to Jim.

For once he appeared at a loss. "You don't have to do that," he protested. "Rudy can manage for a while. I'll call an employment agency in town. They'll have somebody up here in a few days."

Stacey knew it might be more difficult than that to get a qualified chef to live in these remote mountains, even temporarily. "Don't worry about it." She bustled into the kitchen and started pulling cartons of eggs and bacon from the refrigerator and setting them on the counter. "I'm a terrific cook, everyone says so. And I won't mind the work. It'll give me something to do."

Pursing his lips, Jim thought about it for a moment. "Well, all right. Just until Miriam's up and around again."

"Fine. Now can you please leave? You're in the way, and I've got breakfast to get out in less than an hour. You don't want your guests complaining, do you?"

She heard Jim chuckling as he pushed through the kitchen's swinging doors.

For the rest of the day Stacey cooked, directed Rudy and familiarized herself with the utensils and supplies. For lunch she laid out a buffet of cold meats and cheeses and had everyone build their own submarine sandwiches. By dinnertime she'd prepared browned pork chops, simmering in onions and tomato sauce, plus rice and a huge Caesar salad.

Walker ate three helpings.

When he'd put away his second frosted brownie, Stacey felt inordinately pleased. She had no doubts about her culinary ability. Her husband had expected her to know her way around a kitchen, and for years she'd tried to please him—taking gourmet classes, trading recipes with neighbors, experimenting.

Pleasantly exhausted that night as she got ready for bed, Stacey admitted to herself that she had seized the chance to do some work here. Partly to feel useful, and partly to show Walker she could be valuable on the ranch. Cooking for the guests each day would give her a valid reason to stay on.

The following afternoon Walker stepped into the kitchen, asking for a cola. Fishing in the refrigerator for the bottle, Stacey handed it over, expecting him to leave, but instead, he dragged out a cane-backed chair, flipped it around and straddled it. In his palm were a block of half-carved wood and a pocketknife.

She set the cola on the table at his elbow and wiped floury hands on her apron. She'd just finished rolling a crust for a blackberry cobbler. For the life of her, she didn't know what to say to him. He'd eaten at the table each meal, putting away stupendous amounts of her food, yet never saying a word about any of it.

She caught her breath in the most irritating fashion each time he came near. She found her gaze straying again and again to his powerful thighs, broad shoulders and corded forearms. Even the long, tanned column of his neck fascinated her, where his shaven beard gave way to smooth skin.

"Is there anything else?" she inquired at last, disturbed by the direction of her thoughts.

"Naw." Ignoring the cola, he proceeded to whittle at the wood, letting the scraps fall into a small waste can.

"Okay. Well…I hope you like meat loaf. I'm fixing it for dinner." She turned her back and put ground beef, eggs and bread crumbs into a bowl. With clean fingers she kneaded the concoction together.

"I like meat loaf." He whittled some more.

"And scalloped potatoes." What did he want?

"I like potatoes, too."

"Good." Adding parsley and milk and dried onion-soup mix, she continued kneading. Out of the corner of her eye, she noticed he still hadn't touched his drink. If he wasn't thirsty, why had he come in here?

The only sounds in the room were the scraping of his knife and her own movements. She felt awkward, as if it were somehow up to her to carry the conversation. Did Walker wonder about the two of them? Did he think about touching her? "Geoff is doing well, isn't he?" she asked, trying to pull her mind from those thoughts. "I'm not much of a judge, but I noticed he's riding with more confidence."

The cowboy nodded. "Geoff's doing fine."

"By the way, Miriam is recovering nicely from her operation, you know. Jim told me this morning her husband called to report her progress. She should be back to work within six weeks or so." Was she chattering?

Finally, he looked up. "That mean you'll be here till she comes back?"

So busy the past day and a half, Stacey hadn't given herself time to think. In that instant she made up her mind. "Yes. I'll work in the kitchen until Miriam comes back." She packed the meat mixture into several loaf pans, poked them with a fork and set them on the oven's center rack.

Walker stood, pushing back the chair. "Aren't you gonna put any tomato sauce or catsup on the meat loaf? I like it with catsup."

She bristled, but kept her voice even. "I have to cook off all the extra grease first. I won't put on the catsup until it's nearly done. But don't worry, there will be plenty."

"Fine." He moved to the swinging doors and pushed one open.

Hands on hips, she frowned at his back. Had he come in here merely to tell her how to prepare food, for Pete's sake?

Before he went through the doors, Walker paused. Over his shoulder, he said, "I like your cooking. It's pretty good."

"Thank you" was all she could manage to get out on a strangled note. *Pretty good?* Some compliment. It was nothing like the kind of flowery, heartfelt praise she'd imagined would come from a deeply interested man. Here she'd been thinking romantically about his damn neck, and he had nothing on his mind but a block of wood and getting enough catsup!

He was gone.

With a huffy snort, she turned toward the sink to rinse her hands, but something on the table caught her eye. It was the block of wood, now transformed into a perfect horse.

No one had to tell her Walker had made it for her. A gift. She just knew it.

Quickly she washed her hands, dried them and scooped up the charming piece. For several minutes she studied the clean lines of the legs, the graceful back, the proud carriage of the head. It was lovely. Sighing, Stacey set it down again. Only then did she notice the bottle of cola still there. Untouched.

The next day he arrived at close to the same time, in between trail rides, this time asking for something to eat. She glanced at the whittled horse she'd put in a place of honor on the windowsill, then set a plate of peanut-butter cookies on the small table. He pulled out a chair again and straddled it backward.

"Do you always sit like that?" Stacey asked.

He smiled self-consciously. "Guess I've forked a horse for so many years, it's just natural. It bother you?"

She wondered what he'd do if she said it did. "I don't mind."

"These cookies are pretty good," he proclaimed after taking a huge bite. "Peanutty, you know?"

"Thank you." She smiled at him, thinking that perhaps he was trying to be complimentary, though this wasn't quite what she wanted to hear from an admiring male. What she had in mind was maybe more like: *Your hair shines like the glow of the moon. Your eyes sparkle like a sun-kissed lake.*

"But oatmeal raisin are my favorites," he went on while her smile wilted. "Miriam's were great. I sure miss 'em. Can you make those?"

Oatmeal raisin were her specialty. "I guess I could try sometime."

Choosing another cookie, he didn't bother with biting it this time, but put the entire thing into his mouth. As he munched, he let his gaze roam the room with an aimless air, as if he were passing the time.

It wasn't until only crumbs were left on the plate that it occurred to her why he might have come. Since he appeared to have nothing pressing in mind, he might just want simple companionship. Perhaps he was lonely. Walker was human, after all, no matter how hardheaded he sometimes appeared.

Perhaps he just needed to be with someone. Lord knows, she was lonely. How often lately had she wished for a masculine presence to stand beside her, support her, love her? She sighed at the impossibility of it all.

Sliding him a glance, she questioned her earlier conclusions about Walker. He'd told her repeatedly to stay away from him, yet here he was, seeking her out twice in two days.

Could there be a different reason? Walker had told her that if she controlled him, she'd control the ranch. But wasn't the reverse also true? If he controlled her, wouldn't he have free rein here? As matters stood, Walker's motives had to be suspect.

Stacey sighed again, confused, as usual, by her conflicting emotions. If only she had an older brother or sister to confide in. But she'd been an only child, growing up with her quiet parents until her father had died several years back.

At her side, Walker suddenly appeared. She'd half turned away, and deep in her musing, hadn't seen him approach.

He touched her shoulder. "Where'd you ride off to just now?"

"Just thinking."

"About what?"

"Just . . . what I'll do," she improvised.

His gaze flicked over the pile of dirty dishes. "Guess being a cook'll keep you plenty busy."

"That's not what I meant," she said, wondering if he had deliberately misunderstood her. But in his expression she thought she saw something she'd have thought was alien to Walker. She thought she saw caring.

The possibility brought a smile from somewhere deep within. "Besides, don't you know the difference between a cook and a chef?"

"No. What?"

Unable to stop herself smiling, she said, "Chefs don't wash dishes."

He laughed. "That's Rudy's job, eh?"

"Right." Her smile widening, Stacey found she liked the answering humor in Walker's dark face. Setting aside her mistrust of him for a moment, she searched his features, looking for the honesty and integrity she hoped and suspected he possessed.

Yet within seconds she found herself losing sight of that goal and merely enjoying his flashing smile. When he stood over her like this, he made her skin tingle with a heightened awareness she'd never known. A spurt of desire shivered through her. Usually, he didn't wear his hat indoors, but today he did. Beneath it, she knew his hair was thick and silky. Would she ever get the chance to touch it?

The man could have no idea of how incredibly compelling he was. As he studied her face in return, she felt the pull of raw sexuality spread flickers of warmth through her. Walker excited her, made her feel more womanly than any

other man had done, just by looking at her. Slipping unbidden into her mind came images of being gently crushed
in his strong arms.

A breath of his scent filled her nose, and she drew it in.
In her hands she held a spatula, but now her fingers gripped
it tighter. It took her several seconds to realize her hands
were trembling. An aroma of horses and hay and tanned
leather mingled faintly in the air around him. Without his
moving, she felt he had somehow drawn nearer. Her gaze
dropped to his mouth.

With a suddenness that shocked her, she wanted him to
kiss her. Wanted it desperately.

"Don't mess with me, Stacey," he warned her, his eyes
narrowing.

"What do you mean?" In his face she found shrewd in-
telligence, a trace of impatience and a deep, deep hunger.

"Keep looking at me like that," he said in a rough growl,
"and in about five seconds you'll find yourself flat on your
back."

"Oh." Stacey felt her face flood with color, and she put
a hand to the side of her throat. "Sorry."

Playing with fire, that was what she was doing.

Walker was not an innocent boy or even a terribly civi-
lized man. He was a dangerous, unpredictable male animal, and she'd better not forget it.

"I've got to start peeling potatoes," she mumbled, jerk-
ing away to yank open a drawer and hunt through it for a
peeler. Her traitorous hands would not stop trembling.
"You'd best get back to work, too. Don't you have a trail
ride soon? The guests will be waiting."

"Yeah." His all-knowing expression told her he wasn't
fooled by her abrupt dismissal. At the same time she
thought he looked as shaken as she felt. In distracted
movements, he lifted his hat to run quick fingers through his
hair, then set it back on, a gesture she'd seen him perform
before when troubled. "Thanks for the cookies." He turned

at the door, pausing. "Plan something that can cook while you're gone tomorrow afternoon. Geoff wants you on the trail ride."

She looked up from the drawer. "He does?" He hadn't mentioned it before.

"We're gonna hunt the wild horses again. He wants you to see them." From his back pocket he pulled at something that was sticking out. "Here. These will protect your hands."

When he passed them over, Stacey felt the soft calfskin gloves and sent Walker a questioning glance. They were brand-new and just her size, similar to the pair he'd given Geoff. He couldn't have had time to get to town, so whose were they? "Where did you get these?"

He shrugged. "An Indian lady I know over the hill makes them. Couple of days ago I asked her for some about your size." One side of his mouth kicked up. "I noticed you keep your nails painted pink. You don't want your manicure messed up, do you?"

Without waiting for a reply, he pushed through the swinging doors, and Stacey stared after him, clutching the buttery-soft gloves in wonder. Another gift?

Walker headed for the barn and the waiting guests, feeling an unusual smile pulling at the edges of his normally hard mouth. He knew he probably looked like a damn fool, wearing the silly grin, but he couldn't summon the will to wipe it off.

Stacey . . . wanted him?

The possibility sharpened the edge of the sexual frustration he'd been caught in for days. His chest expanded in a deep breath. He hoped she was feeling it, too. He didn't know what it was about him she might be drawn to, or why. After all, he was a basically unsocial man with a flawed face. But he was not about to question his good luck. And for just a few precious seconds he consciously avoided wondering about any underlying motives she might be harboring.

If she wanted to control the ranch through him, she was welcome to try. That would never happen, and he was crazy to worry about it. What he ought to do was enjoy this unexpected and thrilling development to the fullest.

How long, he wondered, would it take to hustle her into his bed?

Stacey centered a huge turkey in the oven, basted it with butter and made sure the stuffing was securely trussed inside before closing the door. Glancing down, she checked her outfit and sighed. No chance anyone would mistake her for a cowgirl. Her jeans were thin and not of riding quality. Her sleeveless blouse was sunflower yellow and knit, not at all like the yoked long-sleeved shirts the other guests wore, but it was the best she could do. The worst part of her outfit was her white tennis shoes. They bore no resemblance to Western boots.

For the first time she wished she'd invested in proper gear before she'd come. Over his breakfast eggs, Geoff had remarked about her ill-suited clothing, and Walker had asked if she intended to ride in them. She'd nodded, embarrassed, then wondered at her reaction. Less than two weeks ago it wouldn't have mattered what Walker thought.

"You need boots," he'd said without preamble. "I'll let you go today because we're just going to walk the horses, but it's not safe, riding without a good heel. I'll put you up on Spot." He chuckled. "That old cayuse wouldn't break into a trot if a mountain lion jumped on his back."

As she cleared plates while the guests wandered out after breakfast, she did some quick calculating. She would soon owe another month's rent on her city apartment, which would dig sharply into her savings. But she and Geoff wouldn't be there to run up the utilities, so she wouldn't have to worry about that, thank goodness. Still, even living here for six more weeks, she couldn't justify the expense of new cowboy boots. They were simply too pricey.

Her gaze dropped, and she could feel her shoulders slumping. She ought to head down to the corrals now; they'd be waiting for her.

With unseeing eyes, she stared at the turkey through the oven's small glass window and wondered at the change in herself. When had she started caring so much about Walker's opinion?

A warm hand curved around her shoulder, yet she wasn't startled. Maybe her thoughts had summoned him. Walker said, "You're not scared, are you?" He leaned forward, as if checking her face. "I didn't mean to frighten you with that talk about mountain lions and such."

She shook her head but hadn't the heart to admit the truth.

Both hands on her bare shoulders now, he squeezed, massaging and molding her skin beneath his palms, sending a sweeping rush of pleasure through her veins that escalated her pulse. His voice was slow and deep. "Don't think about a thing, darlin'. You know I'll take care of you. Real good care." To emphasize his comment, he ran his hands down her arms and chafed her skin, smiling into her face.

She smiled back tremulously. He couldn't possibly realize the implication of his words.

Since she'd already instructed Rudy to get the mashed potatoes ready later and then put in the green-bean casserole, she headed for the corrals with Walker.

Once there, he wasted no time in getting her atop Spot, the Appaloosa gelding she'd ridden before, and steering the procession onto a trail that wound behind the ranch house and into the hills. At first, Stacey was nervous. She hadn't been on a horse since the first day she'd arrived, and still had little idea of how to go about guiding one.

But Walker patiently explained the basic principles of riding, directing her to hold the reins in one fist and reminding her to keep her heels down for better balance.

Stacey grasped the reins as he said, thrust her heels down and looked at him for assurance. He nodded approval. "You're doing fine, honey, just fine. We'll make a cowgirl out of you yet."

It was Walker's calm manner, his confidence that helped her relax. On every side, the Tehachapi Mountains rose up like great, protecting giants. Tall, California oaks gazed kindly down on scrub brush and sage. Brilliant orange poppies appeared even more vivid next to tiny blue lupines. They rode on, and Stacey inhaled, liking the fresh-scented wilderness.

Walker rode up and down the line of guests, politely inquiring about each one's comfort, giving instruction when asked, keeping quiet when not. He seemed the perfect guide, Stacey mused, watching him. Surprising her, he even became talkative when she asked about the cattle she could see close by in the hills.

The brown-and-white coats of Hereford cattle were clearly visible; here a white-faced mama lifted her head when the riders passed by, there a small group of the larger bulls grazed.

"Do you always keep the same type of cow?" Stacey asked. "All Herefords?"

Walker tilted his head. "Once we bought a blooded Brahman bull that cost a bundle. We figured to turn him loose come summer and get a good crop of crosses. But he wasn't cooperating."

"Why not?"

He lifted one shoulder. "Couldn't ever get him to the ranch. The seller lived across the valley, over by the Tehachapi loop—the train tracks—and told me part of the deal was to go get him."

"And did you?"

By his rueful grin, Stacey knew the story was complicated. "I took a couple of our cowboys over there, trailer-
ing our horses, and we set out to find him. The three of us
split up and wouldn't you know, I got lucky—spotted him
halfway up the side of a steep wash. And he was big. I'd
stake my saddle he weighed in at two thousand pounds."

"Wow," Geoff breathed. "How much does a horse
weigh?"

"Let's put it this way, son. That bull'd make at least two
of your horse. Anyway, I figured we had to get up behind
him, haze him down the mountainside and into a corral we
had waiting. But he had other ideas."

Geoff egged him on. "What ideas, Walker?"

Stacey noticed the other riders had stopped, waiting for
them to catch up. When they did, no one wanted to go on,
but listened attentively to Walker's story.

Stacking his hands atop his saddle horn, Walker hooked
one leg over the pommel. She noticed how Geoff watched,
then emulated the wrangler's position.

"He took off at an angle, running straight for the train
tracks." Walker pursed his lips, pausing. "I figured, fine,
he wouldn't stay on them long, but I was wrong. I took after him, running my horse full tilt along those tracks, when
I realized it had become steep mountain on one side and
sheer drop on the other. You had to stay on those tracks
'cause there was no other place to go."

"And?" Stacey found herself as captivated as the rest.

"And that bull just kept running. I didn't worry till I
heard the train coming."

"Uh-oh." Mr. Potter said. "Had you already paid for the
bull?"

"Yep. But he was insured, so I figured it would be the sad
loss of a valuable animal and just moved my horse over as
close to the mountain as I could, until the train passed."
Making a dramatic pause, Walker met each person's eyes
before proceeding.

Stacey smiled; she could tell he was loving this.

"That train finally passed," he continued. "I rode down to see the carcass, and what do you know, but that bull must've got off the tracks like I did, 'cause he was back on 'em again and running away."

"He wasn't killed?" Geoff's eyes were big.

"Not hardly. The chase started up again until he high-tailed it around a hairpin and stopped. That old brute turned to face me and my horse, horns down and ready to hook us. But I didn't know it until I came around the bend and ran into him. Well, he gored my horse, not bad, but enough to draw blood. More scared than anything, my horse went down, with me jumpin' out of the stirrups. There I was, no horse under me, a drop on one side and steep mountain on the other, and a mad, two-thousand-pound bull wantin' to make a pincushion of me."

"What happened?" Mr. Potter asked, his voice boyish and eager.

Walker frowned gravely. "Well, I think of myself as a tough man, but that day I wasn't tough. I turned to that steep bank and clawed my way up, grabbing clumps of weed and handholds of rock faster'n a jackrabbit running from a coyote. All the time that bull was beneath me, butting up with his head and trying his durndest to plant his horns in my rump."

The group laughed, and Potter said, "You must have gotten up high enough, because you don't walk with a limp."

"Yessir. Just high enough, about ten feet, and had to wait up there, clutching an old sagebrush bush until that bull got tired of waiting and wandered off. Took me more than two hours to catch my horse and lead him back for treatment. I never did get that bull." He chuckled. "But I did get my money back."

"And I'll bet to this day you don't like Brahmans, eh, Walker?" Potter concluded.

"You're dead right."

"Look!" Geoff shouted, pointing ahead. "It's the mustangs. Mom, see?"

Stacey shaded her eyes and spotted the distant band. About eight mares, bunched together in the lee of a small draw. But she saw no sign of the stallion.

"Where's Ridgefire?" Geoff wanted to know, echoing her thoughts. She could hear worry in his voice.

Walker nudged his horse up to the boy. "See up the mountainside? He's camouflaged against the hill. Studs like to stay a little apart from their mares to keep a lookout for danger."

"I see him now." Geoff sat back in his saddle, a sigh of relief in his voice. "He's great, huh, Mom? I wish he could be my horse. I'd take really, really good care of him and ride him every day."

A low chuckle escaped Walker. "Nobody rides that horse, boy. He's rank." His tone became regretful. "It's a crying shame, a horse that beautiful becoming such an outlaw."

Mr. Potter frowned. "Out here he's able to bring good bloodlines back into these wild ones, though, isn't he?"

"Sure. He's doing his duty by these mares. And at least he hasn't been slaughtered for dog food."

"Oh, no!" Geoff cried.

Walker shrugged and urged the riders to move on, but Stacey did not miss seeing her son gaze wistfully over his shoulder at the stallion.

The next day, after a conference between Walker and Jim, Walker announced that he would have to send some of the cowboys out to round up at least one of the bands of wild horses.

"There's just too many running those hills now," he explained to everyone at the dinner table. "I have to agree Jim's right about that. If we're gonna let any of them stay, we need to weed some out."

"What will happen to them?" Geoff asked, his spaghetti dinner apparently forgotten.

"They'll be sent to the BLM and hopefully get adopted out." Walker shook his head soberly. "I wish it could be another way."

Unfortunately, Ridgefire was among the captured ones. When the cowboys chased the horses down the mountain and rode up whooping amid dust clouds and thundering hooves, Stacey should have known Geoff would instantly spot the big stallion.

"Hey!" he shouted, running from the house through the rising dust and confusion toward the far corral. "You guys got the wrong ones! You got the wrong—"

"Geoff!" Walker reached out, grabbing hold of the boy's arm before he could charge mindlessly through the rails and into the midst of the panicked herd. From her position on the front porch, Stacey breathed a sigh of relief. She approached the two more slowly. "You can't go in there— you'll get trampled!" Walker admonished Geoff. "Now use your head."

The boy barely heard him, fighting against the strong hold. "They got the wrong ones! They've got to let them go."

"Stop it." Walker gave Geoff a little shake. "Now listen. They had instructions to bring in whichever band was closest to the ranch. It's too bad it was your favorite horse, son, but they're in now, and we won't be letting them go. You'll have to accept it."

The boy quit struggling at last. His eyes were wide and frightened. "Are you gonna let him get killed for dog food?"

"No!" Walker snapped, then gentled his voice and relaxed his grip. "No. First off, Ridgefire isn't truly a wild horse, or even a mustang. So he's not protected by the same laws. He's a registered quarter horse that escaped. We just let him go, that's all. He still belongs to the Bar M."

"You said he's an outlaw. Will you sell him, then?"

Walker dipped his head in the gesture of uncertainty Stacey was coming to recognize. "I don't know. We'll have to see."

The beginnings of a smile formed on Geoff's face.

"Don't start dreaming about him, though. Like I told you, he's rank. He doesn't trust any human, and he'd as soon run you down as look at you. He's dangerous."

"Ridgefire? Dangerous?"

An edge of impatience made Walker's voice abrupt. "I tell you he's gone bad!"

"Walker." Stacey frowned at him, giving him what she hoped was an imperceptible shake of her head.

He sighed and hunkered down beside Geoff. "Look. Some horses are just no good. Maybe his former owner abused him. Maybe he was born vicious, with something wrong in his brain. His type can't be rehabilitated. When we first bought that stud, I worked with him, Geoff. For hours. Days." He flicked a glance at Stacey, who urged him to go on. "I couldn't do anything with him. He was just too far gone. I'm not saying this to blow my horn, but if even I can't make friends with a horse—well, it's as good as can't be done."

Geoff had always been a quiet child, always reasonable, so the mutinous gleam that materialized in his eyes surprised Stacey. "I can make friends with him. I know I can."

Walker stood, making a frustrated sound. "Boy, you gotta understand. If you go against my orders and get in that corral, he could kill you."

"No." Geoff shook his head.

Stacey stepped in. "Geoff, you've got to promise both Walker and me you won't go into that corral. Promise us. Now."

Looking at the two adults he adored, Geoff frowned, and his face fell into the woebegone lines only an unhappy child

can muster. "Okay." He kicked at the ground. "I promise."

Putting a hand upon the boy's head, Stacey smiled.
"You've always kept your word, Geoff. I know you will
now."

He started off toward the corral that held the milling wild
horses and halted well short of the rails, squatting to watch.
Stacey sighed dispiritedly, resting her chin upon her chest.

Standing beside her, Walker heard her sigh and felt at a
loss. He knew she would do anything to protect Geoff from
further heartbreak. He figured he agreed with her; Geoff
had been through enough.

Rising unexpectedly was an urge to reassure her. He
wanted to tell her not to worry, that Geoff would be fine—
he'd see to that.

At his sides his arms hung loosely and felt empty. Seeing
the sun shining upon her bent head, he actually lifted a hand
to touch her hair.

At the last second he caught himself. How often had a
foolish man fallen for a pretty face and a teasing smile? In
truth, he knew very little about the way Stacey thought. But
he should know.

It was time, he figured, straightening, to find out what
Stacey's true motives were. He glanced around. The place
was crawling with guests and their children, cowboys and
animals. Not here. He'd have to get her away.

"I'd like to take you out," he told her in what he hoped
was a mature, straightforward manner. "Away from here,
maybe for a meal."

Her head jerked up, and her mouth formed an O, as if
she'd just swallowed a bug. "Out?" she squeaked.

"Yes. Out." Impatient, he pulled off his hat, raked his
fingers through his hair, then resettled it. This asking for a
date could get embarrassing. What did he have to do, write
out the invitation in the dirt?

Chapter Six

Facing Walker fully, Stacey stared into his eyes. "Let me get this right. You are . . . asking me for a date?"

"Yeah. A date. As in something men and women do together."

"I see." She frowned, wondering what could have presaged this offer. He must truly be getting threatened by her. Could this be about her decision to stay on for the six weeks of Miriam's convalescence? Maybe he was afraid she would move here permanently.

"I see?" he mocked lightly. "You'll go, won't you?"

"I don't think that's a good idea."

"What's not good? We'll drive to town, have a big steak. Talk."

"I can have Rudy pull steaks from the freezer, and we'll all have them for dinner. We can talk here." Go out on a date? She couldn't believe the man was really asking her for something she'd secretly hoped for.

At the same time, she didn't trust that he merely wanted time alone with her. Walker had a complicated mind. He was clever. He must have something up his sleeve. She fastened her eyes on Geoff, still gazing wistfully at the wild horses.

At her side Walker fell silent. She sensed his surprise at her flat refusal, and from the corner of her eye she could see him thrust his hands into the front pockets of his jeans, shoulders high, arms straight.

Stealing a glance at him, she was shocked to discover a flash of hurt in his eyes. He quickly averted his face, but she'd seen it. Had she been wrong?

"I'll look forward to dinner here, then," he told her in curiously deep tones, as if trying too hard to hide his emotions. He spun on his heel and made for the barn. It was where he always went when troubled, Stacey realized.

"Wait." Stacey cursed her mushy heart and took two steps toward him. He stopped, but didn't turn. "I...maybe we could go for a walk or something."

He met her gaze over his shoulder. "A walk?"

"Uh, sure. How about a picnic? I could put together lunch for, say, Saturday? That's only two days off."

"A picnic sounds good," he allowed, relaxing his shoulders a fraction. "But cowboys don't walk."

"No?"

"Cowboys don't walk," he repeated. "They ride." Before he turned away again, she caught the barest suggestion of a smile and called herself all kinds of fool. But she couldn't keep a smile from her own face, any more than he could.

Geoff and Scotty began spending more time together, Stacey was glad to note. And on Friday, a new group of guests arrived and a few others took their leave, their vacations ending. She said a warm goodbye to Mr. Potter and his wife. In the new group were several children close to Geoff's age. Two of them were big boys, twelve-year-old, undisciplined city kids, who ran about the ranch chasing livestock, complaining about the food and demanding the fastest horses.

In less than a day Stacey had had her fill of them and groaned, knowing they'd be at the ranch for a full week. For herself they were a minor annoyance. For Geoff they were major trouble.

After dinner, passing the lounge where guests often congregated to spend the evening playing pool or reading, she caught the two boys taunting Geoff, calling him "short stuff" and "shrimp." Without knowing why, she shrank back from the doorway, keeping out of sight.

Scotty had come up to the big house to play cards after having dinner with his own family. Close to the size of the newcomers, Scotty was not intimidated. "Bug off," he told them. "We're busy."

One of the boys, a redhead, sized up Scotty, who met his stare with a level one of his own. Seeing no fear, the boy turned to Geoff. "Hey, Peewee, we want to play cards. You've had them long enough. It's our turn."

Geoff blinked, and Stacey had to force herself not to interfere. If this situation escalated, as it probably would, she knew her son would give in or start to cry, both reactions he'd displayed before. He said, "There's another deck over there," and pointed across the room toward a rack of games.

"You go get another deck, Peewee. We want this one." The redhead reached out, making a grab for the cards that lay on the table between Geoff and Scotty.

Geoff was faster. His hand shot out, covering the deck. "We're in the middle of a game. You can play when we're finished or get the other deck. Okay?"

Stacey was sure she saw a hint of worry in Geoff's eyes. She bit her lip. "Okay?" he asked again, a plaintive note in his voice.

"No, it's not okay." The boy laid his hand atop Geoff's and squeezed.

"Hey, kid, get lost," Scotty said.

"You get lost," the other boy said to Scotty. "Or maybe you wanna make something of it—out behind the barn?"

Remaining seated, Scotty fumed angrily. "My dad works here. I can't fight the guests."

"Then how about you, Baby?" Redhead taunted, still pinning Geoff's hand. "How about it? Or maybe your mommy won't like it."

A tense silence strung out with three pairs of eyes on Geoff. Even Scotty appeared to be waiting to see how Geoff would handle himself. Stacey bit her lip, forcing herself to keep still. Finally Geoff got to his feet, his face calm. "You're a waste of time," he told the big boys. "Come on, Scotty. Let them have the cards. We can go check out the horses."

With that, Scotty and Geoff vacated their chairs, which the other boys took with triumphant glee. But Stacey was proud. Her son hadn't cried or run away or backed down, not really. He'd simply avoided a brawl and saved face by effecting a dignified exit.

She let out a long breath she hadn't known she was holding and went back into the kitchen. Although it was well past dinner and the kitchen had been cleaned, she put lasagna noodles into a pot of boiling water and started the sauce. When both were finished, she layered them with a ricotta cheese mixture until she had two full pans of lasagna finished and ready to bake for tomorrow's dinner. Rudy had instructions, so she would be able to go on the picnic with Walker.

For a moment her hands lingered over the pans and her mind wandered to the ride tomorrow. Perhaps she could tell him a couple of jokes or compliment him—anything to lighten his usually sober mood. There was a gentleness inside Walker; she knew it. Tomorrow she would start trying to bring it out. If not for herself, then for Geoff's sake. Geoff was growing up fast, and in only a few years he would

be dealing on an adult basis with Walker. She would do it
for Geoff.

"Are we going down into the meadow?" Stacey inquired
as Walker reined in his horse, once they were past the corrals.

"Why? Do you want to go into the mountains?" he returned, flicking her a questioning glance over his shoulder.
He wore jeans, his hat and a mulberry-colored shirt the hue
of dark red wine. As usual, he was settled in the saddle of
his big dapple-gray gelding, and she sat in relative comfort
atop Spot.

"I don't really have a preference. I don't know why, I just
imagined we'd go toward the wild horses." Experimentally,
she squeezed her horse with her legs, and he lengthened his
stride, catching up. "Hey!" she told Walker delightedly,
"that really works, just like you said. I squeezed him and he
went faster."

Walker dipped his head, his hat hiding his eyes for an instant. "You listen to me, Stace. I won't steer you wrong."

They rode stirrup to stirrup. He sat his horse with grace
and strength, absolutely in control, and she admired him, all
long, lean, Stetson-hatted cowboy. "Yes, you'll take care of
me, won't you, Walker?"

Slowly he turned to meet her eyes, and his stare burned
like slow coal. "In every way," he told her simply. And she
could read a wealth of meaning in his comment.

His eyes grew warmer.

Blushing, she averted her face, wondering when she'd
gone from teasing him to flirting with him. What had gotten into her today? Her own clothing was plain and un-
Western. She wished her short-sleeved top was yoked,
wished she had real cowboy boots.

Breaking the silence, he patted the saddlebags tied on the
back of his horse. "I'm glad you packed us a good lunch,

'cause it's at least an hour's ride to where I want to take you.''

"Where are we going?"

He glanced right, then left; it was the gesture of someone who didn't want to be overheard, which was ridiculous, considering they were already a hundred yards down the trail from the ranch. Putting a finger to his lips, he stage-whispered, "An Indian camp."

"Really?" She arched her brows. "Will I get to meet them?"

"Can you speak to the dead?"

"What?"

"Ghosts. Where we're going is an old ghost town of an Indian camp. The last time they camped there was a hundred years ago. All that's left is their spirits. And a few clues to mark their lives."

"Ooh," Stacey breathed, hoping she sounded suitably impressed. "Ghosts. I hope they're not hostile."

"Not to me, they're not. You see, my grandmother, and her mother before her, traded with them. We've always had peace with the Piutes."

Stacey gasped, hearing only part of his statement. "Oh, Walker, you mean this land goes that far back in your family? I didn't know...."

"Sure." He nodded, guiding his horse around a small boulder. "In fact, I'm the fifth generation in the Marshall family to live and work the Bar M."

Of course he wouldn't want the property to pass into other hands, she realized, amazed at his lineage. It explained his fierce desire—no, need—to keep the title to these mountains. This land was truly his heritage, truly in his blood.

He was talking again. "Someday I'd like to see the land go to my sons."

"You'll have to get married first," she informed him, trying to keep her tone light. She fussed with the collar of her short-sleeved blouse, smoothing the sky-blue cotton fabric which, she knew, matched her eyes. "Have you considered that?"

He inclined his head. "Not too much, actually. But I am thirty now. Guess I should give some thought to taking a wife. Somebody strong—to give me strong sons."

"Yes," Stacey whispered, wild, disjointed thoughts filling her mind. She saw herself big with Walker's baby. With his son.

She glanced at him and was jolted to find his speculative glance on her midriff. Had he read her mind? The surprise shot sparks down to her toes. For something to do, she made a show of arranging the leather reins in her left hand. The gloves Walker had given her were soft and did indeed protect her uncallused palms. She should thank him for his thoughtfulness.

"These gloves are wonderful. I really like them."

Walker shrugged. "It's nothing." His saddle creaked, and Stacey glanced at it. The attractive tan color showed intricate tooling and bits of silver trim. "Your saddle is different from the others, isn't it? It's really pretty."

He rubbed his hand over the leather with great satisfaction. "It's a Billy Cook Roper—double cinched to hold me on the horse when I'm roping. The horn sits up a mite higher than on other saddles, so I can use it for cutting competitions or for just plain work."

"Your pride and joy?" she asked, feeling perceptive.

"Sure is." Their eyes met, and they both smiled.

They rode on, with Walker pointing out interesting landmarks and the occasional animal. They spotted hawks circling overhead and once a coyote stopped to watch them pass. At last, they came to an outcropping of rocks at the base of the mountain. Stacey saw a stream tinkling over smooth stones and around bends, the clear water pooling prettily in the hollows.

"Oh!" she cried. "This is lovely."

"Like it?" Walker asked. "This is the Indian camp." He dismounted, hobbled his horse and came around to her. She was still aboard Spot, wondering how to dismount without landing in a disgraceful heap. Already she was a little sore. She didn't see any mounting blocks around.

Walker put his hands around her waist. "Here, I'll help. Bend your right leg over the saddle, and I'll ease you off."

She nodded, automatically steadying her hands on his shoulders. Through his shirt she could feel his sun-warmed skin and the flex of his powerful shoulder muscles and let her fingers curl into his strength.

"That's it," he said, guiding her off the horse. She supposed it was only the natural force of gravity that caused her body to glide in excruciatingly slow inches down the entire length of his. She felt the slight friction of her clothing against his, felt his belt buckle skim her stomach. Lastly, she became aware of the soft fullness of her breasts as they slid across his chest.

By the time her toes touched solid ground, she could hardly breathe. "Thank you," she managed to whisper.

Walker stared into Stacey's wide blue eyes and felt himself going under. Well, he'd done it to himself, deliberately sliding her lush body against his so he could at last feel her shape. He gritted his teeth. Beneath his fingers her waist was small and taut, her faint violet fragrance drifting around him and filling his senses like a seductive cloud.

Damn it! This was no time to imagine how her lips would feel beneath his own, how her breasts would fill his palm. He wanted her...willing and warm and susceptible to him. Surrendering sweetly...

With a rough jerk, he pulled away from her and set about loosening the horses' cinches. He'd best remember that he'd brought her out here for a specific purpose, to discover her true plans for the Bar M. Did she figure to start participating in business decisions? Did she think she could sashay in here and change the way things were done—the way he did things?

After he had some answers, maybe then he'd try his luck with the lady. He already knew she was drawn to him, at least in some ways. Maybe later he could start pushing past her meager defenses and get her beneath him, where she belonged.

Yes, that was where the beautiful widow belonged. Beneath him. Walker smiled grimly to himself and finished with the cinch.

Looking over Spot's withers, he saw Stacey carry the saddlebags to a flat, grassy area and begin laying out a navy plaid blanket. She sat down, folding her legs gracefully, and paused, looking around. Her dark hair swung against her cheek, and she smiled softly. "Oh, Walker, I don't care if there are ghosts here. They must be friendly, as you said, because it's the most peaceful spot I've ever seen."

Even from across the clearing he could feel her happiness. Watching her, his mood lightened. The woman was unfailingly good-humored, a trait he didn't understand. But he didn't have to understand her to appreciate her. All these qualities a man could admire—good mother, hard worker, warm to everyone. Even to him, and he hadn't been exactly courteous.

Surprising himself, he guessed he did like Stacey. He hoped to corral more of that warmth for himself. Much more. Maybe...maybe she could learn to like him, too.

Feeling strangely humble, he walked toward her with mixed emotions. He'd have to get himself under control, begin interrogating her, demand the truth. Now. The time was now.

"Fried chicken all right?" she asked, glancing up, the innocence in her eyes irritating him.

"Yeah." He sat down. They were alone at last. He began formulating his plan of attack.

"There's also potato salad, oranges, a thermos of iced tea and cookies." Clearly oblivious of his intentions, she carefully arranged a large plate of food for him and handed it over with a gingham napkin and a smile. He took it and his frown deepened.

The chicken was crispy on the outside and juicy on the inside. The potato salad was seasoned just right, not too salty, and while he ate, she set aside her own food and began peeling an orange for him, even sectioning it.

He savored the food and watched her eat her own, finding it difficult to believe that Stacey was going to all this effort for him. At her elbow was a plastic container of cookies. She saw him glance at them and said, "Oatmeal raisin. I remember you said you liked them."

"I do." He put down his chicken and studied her. Very soon he would get some answers. But her manner distracted him. He'd never had anyone care what kind of food he liked or extend themselves to please him. The experience was confusing. And he was afraid—afraid it wouldn't last. "When did you have time to bake them? And fry this chicken?"

"Oh, last night."

"After dinner? You must've been up late. You shouldn't have gone to so much trouble."

She blushed and waved off his comment.

"Stacey." He wiped his mouth and tried to capture her glance. "What did you do about dinner for tonight? We'll be back in time to eat, but not for you to fix it. Is Rudy cooking?"

She nodded. "I told him exactly when to put in the lasagna, don't worry. It's all taken care of."

"Lasagna? You made that last night, too?" He was astounded. She must have been up half the night, baking and cooking, all so that she could come out with him on this simple picnic.

Thinking hard, he stared at a far-off mountain peak. He hadn't realized, when he'd asked her on the ride today, that she would have to do so much preliminary work just to be able to come along. But she'd arranged it all without complaining or even mentioning it.

She must really want to be with him.

He needed to ask her his questions, he really did. Yet even as he reminded himself of this, it seemed more important that nothing interrupt the smooth flow of camaraderie between them. If he was honest, he knew getting the answers instantly wasn't urgent. Tomorrow or next week would do.

Today he wanted Stacey smiling at him, as she was now, lulling him, almost drugging him with her caring.

"Are you finished eating?" he asked, the solicitude in his own voice surprising him.

She put aside her plate. "Sure."

"Come on. I want to show you something." Together they put everything back into the saddlebags. When it was all packed away, he stood, taking her hand and drawing her to her feet. He threaded her fingers through his, led her toward the stream and was pleased when she came willingly. As if following his lead was the most natural thing in the world.

He'd come here many times as a child and even as an adult, seeking solace from a cold world. Often he'd found it, if only temporarily. Today he wanted to share it with Stacey.

From rock to rock they jumped over the water to where the stream eddied in tiny rivulets around barriers of small boulders. Once past the fall line of the stream, where it was dry, Walker sat on a flat shelf, pulling Stacey into the spot beside him. The warmth of the sun and Stacey's smile brought a pleasant lassitude that spread through him. A breeze whispered by, cooling the dry sunlight, and soothed his skin like feminine fingers.

Walker shook his head to shake off his fanciful thoughts. Knees bent, boot heels on the ground before him, he dug sand from a three-inch hole in the rock. "See? This is where the Piutes ground corn for a kind of bread."

"Like a mortar and pestle? Yes, I see." She collected an elongated rock and began digging sand from another such hole. "This is incredible. They actually lived here, didn't they? It's hard to believe until you see physical evidence. It's exciting."

"Well, I don't know about exciting," he drawled, amused by her enthusiasm. "But it's kinda interesting, I guess." He liked the way she was enjoying this spot he cherished. The early afternoon sun colored her skin with a healthy glow, and her bright blue eyes sparkled. She was smiling, digging into the rock like a little kid. A bit of her hair caught on her lips, and she pulled it away with a slow, unconsciously sensual movement that took his breath away.

"I don't bring the guests here on trail rides," he said gruffly. "I like to keep it, you know, special."

She stopped abruptly. "You mean, I'm the only other person you've brought here?" At his nod, she grasped his upper arm, and her face grew serious. "Then I'm honored, Walker. This place will always be special to me, too."

Stacey's guileless touch ignited the flame he'd carefully tried to keep banked all day. He looked at her pink-tipped fingers touching his body, caressing him. Even though she only held his arm, that didn't stop his mind from conjuring up other places he yearned for her to touch. As much as he wanted that, he wanted his hands on her even more.

He reached to capture her wrist, his fingers closing around the delicate bones in a fierce, possessive grip. "Stacey," he said, low and quietly desperate. "Stacey!"

For the life of her, Stacey couldn't move. She heard the stark need in his voice as clearly as she heard the tinkling of the stream behind them. Her heart rate, never steady around him, doubled. His hazel, dark-fringed eyes blazed, communicating his desire for her like the burning of a red-hot brand.

He released her wrist and lifted his knuckles to graze her cheek, his gentle touch belying the fire alight in his eyes.

Don't think, a voice whispered inside her. *Don't think about the future or his intentions.* It was easy, right now, to listen to that tempting voice. With Walker's strong hands caressing her, everything became simple. *He wants me,* the voice promised, *not the ranch. Me!* Stacey sighed, and with the tiniest movement imaginable she nuzzled his hand. She'd never known green-flecked eyes like Walker's could grow so heated. But they were hot now. Blast-furnace hot.

His knuckles slid down until his strong, callused hand cupped the back of her neck, and his thumb rested on the uneven pulse at the base of her throat. "I'm glad you like it here," he said, his voice low and husky. "But you can give me something even more special to remember when I come back."

"What?" The word caught in her throat, then whooshed out in an escape of pent-up emotion.

"A kiss." The lines of his face were taut with tension, sexual desire and something else it took her a moment to identify.

Uncertainty.

Walker wasn't sure she would consent to his embrace. The big, tough cowboy was actually worried he might rebuff him.

She could see he was waiting while she considered his request. Very still. Tense. Unsure. Longing. And this last idea made her want to throw herself into his arms.

For a long second her eyelids drifted closed, and she felt her lips curve into a promising smile. Overhead, the sun felt sultry and good. Scents of pine and wildflowers flowed down the mountain, over the streambed, surrounding her. Saying nothing, she opened her eyes and nodded.

The cowboy angled his face, his hat shading her features an instant before his mouth covered hers. Stacey remained perfectly quiet. She didn't know what she expected from Walker—rough passion, a fast taking of her mouth by storm or a violent, needful embrace.

But she never did expected this tentative tenderness.

As he carefully rubbed his lips over hers, her heart filled. Here was the gentleness she knew him capable of. Here was the tender, considerate man hidden beneath the layers of bitterness. Against his mouth, she sighed his name.

Nibbling along her lower lip, he seemed in no hurry to escalate the embrace. Beneath the hair at her nape, his hand massaged her skin; his thumb traced delicate patterns on her throat. His sensitivity filled her with wonder, and she leaned closer.

His mouth drifted to kiss the spot just below her ear. She lifted her chin, arching to give him access, feeling a powerful feminine need to please and be pleased. Moving tentatively, she placed her hands on his arms, then slid them over his wine-dark shirt, learning the hard contours of his muscled shoulders. He was so strong. So capable and tough. Yet now he exhibited amazing restraint; she knew it by the faint trembling of his hand.

He wanted more, she could sense it vibrating in every fibre of his being. Much more. The knowledge of her own allure for him made her spirit soar, spreading delicious warmth through her veins.

Walker kissed her again, this time more deeply; a melding of tongues and the damp taste of need. Stacey moved her hands to his head, spearing her fingers into his hair, dislodging his hat and knowing he didn't notice when it tumbled to the ground. She had ample evidence of his desire now, but a part of her wanted more—she didn't exactly know what. An avowal of affection? A declaration? Could she test him, just a little?

"Walker," she breathed against his lips, "do you like me to touch you here?" Thrust deep in his hair, her fingers stroked his scalp.

"Sure." He kissed her chin, her cheek.

"But perhaps you'd rather I did this." She allowed her palms to curve around his shoulders and down his back.

He pulled away a fraction, but didn't release her, a grin playing around his mouth. "Darlin'," he drawled, "you can touch me anywhere you like. Anywhere."

"Thank you," she returned.

He chuckled. "Don't mention it. But you were teasing me. Turnabout's fair play."

Stacey blinked, a suggestion of danger creeping into her consciousness. For a moment, their kissing had been wonderful in itself. But Walker wasn't playing games, she told herself. He was deadly serious. What had she expected, for heaven's sake!

She said. "Um, I don't think we should—"

"Shh." He pressed her close, enfolding her in a hug, patting her back. "Don't fret, sweetheart. I'm not gonna push you into anything you don't want. I'll just hold you, pet you...like one of the horses."

She reared back an inch and smiled into his face. "Walker, I'm not one of your horses you can wave your magic wand over, or whatever it is you do to charm them."

"No, you're not a horse," he agreed, grinning. "But you are a little like one of my mares. If I talk sweet to you, you'll come to me, won't you?"

"Walker." She said his name warningly.

He kissed her nose. "Yes, darlin'?"

"Quit." It was a word she'd heard him use with the horses.

"Anything you say." His grin faded and his expression sobered. "Kiss me again." This was no request, no plea, but a masculine demand, and Stacey was helpless; she couldn't refuse.

"Yes," she said. "Yes."

This time it was her hands that trembled. When his mouth came down on hers and his tongue sought entrance, she felt the tension building in him and in herself. He pulled her close until her breasts were crushed against the hard wall of his chest. They grew heavy, as if weighted, their peaks hardening. A new heat that lay curled tightly in her belly began blooming, like a flower opening to the sun. It sent intermingling messages of hope and pleasure such as she'd never known.

He tucked her head into his shoulder, still kissing her, then lifted his face, staring down. "I've wanted this," he whispered gruffly. "For so long. I don't think you can imagine how I've ached for you."

Stacey smiled, thrilling to his words. "Have you?"

"Since you came, I've hardly been able to sleep. I've been—" he shifted position on the rock "—a mite uncomfortable." Suddenly he grinned. "Maybe I should buy a bigger pair of jeans."

Gasping, Stacey bit her lip. Things were getting out of hand. The danger she'd sensed before set off warning bells in her head. Reaching up to cup his hard cheek, she said, "Walker? I don't mean to lead you on. That is, I mean . . . kissing is one thing, and that's all right. But . . ."

"Yes?"

He wasn't going to make this easy for her. "Uh, I don't want you to get the idea that I'll . . ." Words failed her and she groped, at last drawing herself up, as much as his embrace would allow. Primly she said, "Walker, I'm a principled woman. I don't sleep around."

"You mean I won't have any competition?"

"No! Walker, you don't under—"

"Hush, baby." He put a callused finger on her lips. "I know what you mean, I'm just teasing. Can't you tell?"

Walker, teasing?

"I told you I won't push you into anything," he said. "Believe me?"

"Yes, but—"

"Then quiet, woman. All I want right now is some satisfying kissing. At least—I'm willing to settle for just that. For now. All right?"

"All right." She felt humbled by his chivalry, ridiculously pleased. Smiling into his eyes, she knew that the deep feelings she was beginning to have for him shone on her face.

He kissed her again. Again. It didn't take long to wonder if she and Walker could have a real relationship. Man to woman. Long-term.

Suddenly, Stacey knew Walker could give her stability. He had the power to make her heart whole, as no expanse of dirt and mountains ever would. This half-civilized man with the strange affinity for horses could be The One.

He'd hinted that he cared for her. Would imagining a future for them be too illogical, too crazy?

She didn't know. Kissing him back was all she could think of now, all she wanted in the world. When he levered an arm behind her and laid her down on the rock, she didn't resist. She couldn't. All she wanted was to get closer, and with her arms wrapped tightly around his back, she wriggled slightly, seeking more contact, more of Walker. The movement dragged her sensitized breasts across his chest, and they both gasped. She kissed him back with all her heart.

Suddenly she heard low hoofbeats. Two riders bore down on them, and a child's voice called out to her. Walker abruptly sat up. When Jim and Geoff came abreast of the rock shelf, she was completely surprised. Both males wore near-comical expressions of shock.

Stacey froze.

"Mom!" Geoff exclaimed, pulling his horse to a halt some feet away. "Why is Walker all wrapped around you?"

Still on his big bay horse, Jim snorted.

"Why, Mom?" the boy persisted.

Stacey put both hands against Walker's chest and pushed. She jerked herself free and stood, shaking. Before she could say anything, Geoff's face was suddenly transformed into lines of delight. "I know! Is it because you're gonna marry Walker? Are you, Mom? Are you?"

Chapter Seven

"No!" Stacey snapped, then tried to soften her tone. "No, Geoff, this doesn't mean Walker and I will marry." She stepped off the shelf and moved to stand by his horse, wanting to touch him, but her hands were shaking so, she was afraid he'd notice. Instead, she twined her fingers together. "Son," she explained as gently as she could, "kissing doesn't necessarily mean marriage."

"Oh" was all he said, clearly confused.

Suddenly, Jim burst out, "Of course not!" He settled his fierce glare upon Walker. "Remember, you're practically brother and sister. You can't marry."

"Who said anything about marriage?" Walker stood, feet braced wide, but remained on the small rock. Stacey saw his hands were fisted, his jaw clenched tight. He stooped to pick up his hat, dust it off on his thigh and jam it onto his head. "Anyway, Stacey and I aren't related at all. Not by blood."

Jim leaned his arm on the saddle horn and rested his other forearm atop that. With one big thumb he nudged his pearl-gray hat onto the back of his head. "Well," he drawled, "sometimes blood's thicker than water, and sometimes not. Margaret used to say—"

"What do you know about my mother?" Walker shouted, startling Stacey. All at once he looked wild, facing his stepfather with antagonism and bitterness. "You never spent time with her! You barely knew her. And when you were with her, you weren't a good husband."

"Don't you criticize me, boy. I took care of her, you hear?"

"No." Walker shook his head. "She was frail, sensitive. You overwhelmed her, you were too strong for her. She couldn't survive with you."

Stacey stared at Walker, amazed at the fury passing between the two men. It occurred to her that she should get Geoff out of there; he was listening with a child's fascination. She reached up to collect his reins and lead his horse away.

"Your mother needed a strong man when I married her," Jim bellowed. "She needed someone tough enough to bring this ranch back from the edge."

Walker scowled warily, shoulders stiff. "Edge of what?"

Without breaking eye contact with Walker, Jim pointed his chin at Stacey. "She knows."

Stacey held up her free hand. "Don't get me involved. I don't want any part of your awful argument. I'm taking Geoff back to the ranch."

"Wait." Walker jumped off the rock and put himself directly into her path. The bright sunlight, so warm and soothing when she'd been in his arms, now glared into her eyes, just as he was doing now. A tiny part of her withered inside. "Tell me," he insisted harshly. "Edge of what?"

She hauled in a breath and accepted the fact that he wasn't going to let her by until she answered. "Jim told me this ranch was close to bankruptcy when he married your mother. Now let go of my arm. You're hurting me." Was this the same, gentle man who'd carefully stroked her moments ago? She frowned at his stunned expression. "You really didn't know?"

"Bankruptcy? But we've always had plenty of cattle, plenty of water and feed. We started the guest ranch—"

"That same year," Jim finished. "The guest facility was added to subsidize the ranch. Beef prices were dropping, this area was in the middle of a five-year drought, the place was in foreclosure—gonna go to the bank, for sure." He straightened in his saddle. "But I married your mother, and as she wanted, worked hard to turn this place profitable again. I've done a damned good job."

Walker paled. Some of his fury appeared to drain away, leaving not relief, Stacey decided, watching him with concern, but a kind of defeat. Traces of anger lingering in his closed fists, he turned away and walked like a blind man toward the waiting horses. He led Stacey her mount, helped her up with impersonal hands and swung aboard his big gray. All without a word. Stacey watched him, troubled by his obvious shock. As they rode together back to the ranch, she guessed it was best to let him digest this information without interruption. He didn't speak to her or anyone else for the rest of the day.

"Help me understand, then," Stacey entreated Jim in his office the next morning. "Why are you and Walker constantly at one another's throats? Don't you realize how lucky you are to have each other? You two should get along."

Seated in his swivel chair behind the messy desk, the big man glanced out the window, and if Stacey hadn't known better, she could have sworn a sheepish expression crossed his lined face. "I guess, it's just...I can't explain. Walker and I always did rub each other the wrong way."

"Why, Jim?" Stacey persisted, determined to get to the bottom of this. "When he was a boy, did he constantly disobey you? Was he lazy or trying to avoid his work?"

"Oh, no." Jim met her gaze. "He sassed me a lot, but never avoided work—at least there's that. He carried his weight." He chuckled, remembering. "Matter of fact, the opposite's true. The kid was always underfoot, wanting to do more, learn more. Did I ever tell you what he did the time I broke my hip in a tractor accident?"

"No," she murmured, relaxing in her chair. This was good, what she wanted. Perhaps if Jim talked long enough about his relationship with Walker, she'd pick up some clues. "Tell me about it."

"Well, I was laid up some. This was about, oh, fifteen to twenty years ago, when Walker was barely a teenager. After a few weeks of being cooped up in the house, I got it into my head that I wanted to ride. 'Cept, a'course, with that hip, I couldn't mount my horse. I had a big palomino then, named Trouble."

"Uh-huh." Stacey eyed him shrewdly. "Did the doctor actually say you were allowed to ride?"

"Um, not exactly." He chuckled again. "And Margaret stopped me. At least for a few more weeks. But by that time I was going crazy with cabin fever and decided, come hell or high water, I was going to ride. Walker had retrained Trouble."

"To do what?"

"Well, the horse was always one to be restless when I got on him, wouldn't stand still. And he balked a bit when I asked certain things of him. That's why we called him Trouble."

"And—" she was getting impatient "—what did Walker do?"

"Trained him to kneel so's I could get on. Taught him to come when called, walk slower. Other things."

"Each of them designed to make it easier on you, Jim?" she inquired lightly.

He shrugged, nonchalant. "I guess so." He rubbed his shoulder. "Had to rename the horse, though. Wasn't much trouble after Walker got through with him."

Stacey blew out a breath, ruffling her bangs. Some of the hurt and confusion she'd felt since Walker had closed up on her began to dissipate. Walker did nice things for people, but never claimed credit or thanks.

Walker was a good man; the idea was rapidly becoming a certainty in her mind. He spent countless, patient hours with Geoff, brought her small, unusual gifts. Maybe they weren't sachets or roses. But they were gifts from his heart. How silly she'd been, wanting generic things any ordinary, unimaginative man could offer. Walker's presents were practical, useful. Personal.

And he did care for Jim. She didn't know how she knew this, but somehow...she did. So right now, while Jim was feeling charitable about him, she'd best seize the opportunity. "Wouldn't it be fair if you were to do something nice for him? It might help your relationship. Help you both get along better."

He frowned. "Maybe. What did you have in mind?"

Struggling to contain her excitement, Stacey smiled. "Oh, I don't know of anything specific. What do you think?"

Visibly at a loss, Jim shrugged again. Stacey would have laughed at the big man's bewildered expression if the question hadn't been so important. Still fumbling, he said, "I guess...I don't know. He's good with the horses, I'll give him that."

"Fine, then. Have you ever told him you thought so?"

"No."

"Why don't you compliment him? Tell him you appreciate his hard work. Let him see you admire him, at least for that."

Jim rubbed his jaw. "I don't know."

She rose. "Go on. It won't kill you. I promise."

He got up, coming around the desk to take her arm. "I suppose you're good for me, gal. Keep me in line. I'm glad you'll be living here."

"Now, Jim." Instantly on her guard, she corrected him. "I said I had decided to stay until Miriam is well. I'll decide the rest later."

"Sure you will." He pulled her hand through his arm and patted her fingers. "Sure you will."

After dinner, the guests wandered into the lounge, but Jim waited until Walker threw his napkin onto the table and rose. With Stacey standing at the fireplace, Jim said to Walker, "You got them wild horses shipped off yet?"

Walker paused near the door. "Half of 'em, anyway. The BLM's gonna pick up the rest we got penned next week."

"Good job."

Walker nodded absently, reaching for the doorknob. Behind his back Stacey signaled to Jim, nodding insistently toward Walker.

Jim nodded back. "Uh, Walker?" he said. "I saw you working last week with Dan Fowler's nasty gray—the one that kept falling over backward?"

"Well, he wasn't nasty. Just got a bad idea in his head. That's all."

"Anyway, did you get him over it?" Jim asked. To Stacey's keen eye he appeared unsure, his hands hanging awkwardly at his sides. That was fine. He was trying, and that was what counted. Now, if only Walker would respond. Jim continued. "I saw you working with him for quite a while."

"But I didn't take any time away from the guests or our own horses," Walker defended himself quickly. "When I help somebody on the side, it doesn't affect the Bar M."

"I didn't say it did." Jim planted one brawny fist on his hip. "But if I was gonna worry about you shirkin' your work, I'd be complaining about those wild broom tails you got such a soft spot for."

"Well, somebody's gotta worry about them," Walker flared. "You sure don't give a hang about them."

Stacey thought it was time to intervene. "Walker."

"No, and why should I?" Jim returned, ignoring Stacey, who was frantically shaking her head at him. Her heart sank. Would these two always be suspicious of one another? Jim carried on. "All those scrawny studs do is come around and try to steal my mares! At least we got back that quarter horse you let go. He was the worst!"

"Jim..." Stacey tried again to catch his eye, amazed at how fast things could deteriorate between the two men.

"Ridgefire jumped a six-foot fence," Walker said. "I didn't let him go. And he won't try jumping it again because we got his mares penned with him."

"What a relief."

"Glad you feel that way." Walker yanked the door open. "Just leave the horse care to me. You mind the guests."

As Walker prepared to slam out, Jim scoffed at him, and Stacey bit her lip, then suddenly lost her temper. "Oh!" she cried, exasperated. "You're both stubborn fools!" she said as she made a headlong rush for the kitchen.

Geoff was tanned dark as a berry, Stacey thought, watching her son energetically rake leaves from under a shading California oak. Two other boys piled them into plastic bags. Geoff's health and happiness were the results of this outdoor life; he even seemed taller somehow, though they'd only been on the ranch a matter of weeks. Perhaps he was a bit heavier, too. Sunshine, exercise... and Walker's attention were doing wonders for her son.

She sighed, conflicting emotions swirling in her breast. Geoff was doing so well. Yet her relationship with Walker seemed to have reached an impasse. Ever since he'd kissed her in the meadow almost a week ago, he hadn't approached her, nor made mention of their embrace.

But she felt his eyes following her.

Usually they looked directly and carried a message of banked desire. She saw memories of their luxurious kisses in their depths.

At other times his gaze was troubled, as if he didn't know quite what to do about her. That was fine. She didn't know what to do about him, either.

She sighed again. Geoff skipped over, grabbing her hand. "We're gonna check on Ridgefire. You can come, too."

"I can, huh?" she teased, swinging his hand. She'd put a sheet-sized carrot cake into the oven, and it would have to bake for over an hour. Lunch was finished and dinner had been started. She decided she had plenty of time to spend with Geoff.

Behind them, waiting for her answer, were Billy and another boy. "Son," she bent down and whispered, "aren't you going to introduce me to this boy?"

"Sure. This is Ted. He's a guest—came in today when that ratty redhead kid and his friend left. Ted's my buddy. Billy's, too." Geoff pulled Ted forward and presented him. The boy was small for his ten years; he was freckled and sported a big smile.

"Hi," he said shyly.

"Hi, yourself." Stacey shook his hand with all due ceremony. "Welcome to the Bar M. I'm glad you're Geoff's friend. I think you'll like it here. We've got the best food this side of the Mississippi."

Billy giggled, and Geoff grimaced. "Aw, Mom." He grinned at his new friend. "She always says that. She's the cook." He began to trot off, the others at his side.

"The chef," she called after them, knowing it was useless. At the horse pasture she caught up with them and enjoyed Ted's look of wonder and Geoff's look of pride when they saw Ridgefire.

"Isn't he great?" Geoff enthused to the other boys. "He's the bestest horse ever!"

"Best horse ever," Stacey corrected indulgently.

"And someday I'm gonna ride him," Geoff said.

"Really?" Ted's eyes grew wide, and Billy frowned.

"I don't think so." Billy stuck a blade of grass between his teeth. "Walker said he's no good."

"Well, I am gonna ride him."

Stacey knew her frown matched Billy's. She watched her son's small chin come up. "Geoff." She laid a hand on his head. "You remember your promise to Walker and me?"

The boy gazed stonily into the corral. "Yes."

After a moment she said, "All right, then."

He stepped forward, pulled great bunches of overgrown green grass—grass that was out of reach of the horses—and pushed it through the rails. He called to the stallion, who was pacing nervously on the far side. Geoff called again. The horse ignored him.

"You see how his back is turned—" Walker approached from the barn, stopping beside Geoff "—but his ears are flicked back toward you?"

"I see it," Geoff said.

"That means he knows we're all here, but he's insulting us. Won't give us the time of day, so to speak." He knelt and placed a hand upon Geoff's shoulder. "Sorry, son. But I've told you before, he's unsalvageable. A rogue."

Geoff pursed his lips stubbornly.

"He's gone bad, and there's no redeeming him." A note of impatience rang through Walker's tone. "Sooner or later, you'll have to accept it."

The boy stood his ground. "Well, maybe sooner or later he'll want me to pet him."

Walker shook his head. "Jim wants to give him to the BLM next week, and I'm of a mind to agree with him."

"No," Geoff wailed, his face crumbling instantly. "You can't. I'll tame him, I swear. Don't give him away."

Glancing up, Walker met Stacey's gaze, and she frowned worriedly. Once again she wanted to enfold her boy in her arms and kiss everything all right. But with his friends watching, she resisted. He was already on the verge of tears; she couldn't humiliate him now.

Stepping up to Walker, Stacey touched his shoulder. "Do you have to get rid of Ridgefire now? Would it be possible to keep him a while longer?"

"It won't make any difference." The cowboy stood, staring into her eyes. As he rose, Stacey's hand slid off his shoulder and came to rest on the warm, bare skin of his corded forearm.

"Maybe it will. If only to show Geoff you're correct." She squeezed his arm, communicating her request through her eyes and her touch. If flirting had even the tiniest chance of softening the wrangler's heart, she was not averse to using it. For Geoff, of course. "Please."

The muscles beneath her fingers flexed, and Walker's eyes took on a speculative gleam. He tipped his hat back, drawling, "Well, now, I don't guess we need to get rid of old Ridgefire just yet."

Before he could say another word, Geoff whooped and the other boys followed suit, dancing around the grass in little jigs.

"But—" Walker held up a hand "—you'll all give the same promise Geoff has. No going into the corral."

"We won't," they sang out, then dashed toward the barn to get ready for the afternoon trail ride.

Stacey watched them go while Walker chuckled. She let her hand fall away, surprised at her reluctance to break physical contact with him. "Thank you, Walker. I'm grateful you'll keep Ridgefire."

He put a long index finger beneath her chin. "It's quite a favor you've asked. We'll have to feed that horse expensive hay each day—can't turn him out, 'cause he'd figure a way to run off. And we won't be able to use this corral for anything else while we have him."

"You're very generous. Thank you again."

"Not good enough," he said, surprising her. He glided his finger across her cheek and captured a strand of her silky hair. For a moment he seemed distracted by its gloss, rubbing it between his fingers before he smoothed it behind her ear.

"Wh-what do you mean, not good enough?" It was the craziest thing, but whenever he touched her, she felt rooted to the ground, mesmerized, unable to move.

"I mean . . . I want more than your gratitude. Something tangible."

"Well . . . what is it?" Her thoughts scattered. All she understood at the moment was the feel of Walker's hand caressing her face.

"A small thing." His voice was low, husky, taking on the crooning tone he used to calm the horses, she thought. A lambent light in his eyes seemed to call to her. He moved closer, putting both hands against the sides of her neck, letting his palms flatten on her collarbones and his fingers splay over her skin. "A kiss, Stacey. You'll give me that, won't you? To keep Ridgefire?"

"No." She blinked, her lids feeling heavy with a sensuality she wanted to fight. Who did he think he was to keep his distance for days, then turn on the charm? She refused to think that her flirting was in any way responsible. She would simply refuse him. "I won't kiss you for a horse."

"How about for your son? Keeping the horse is making him happy, after all."

Frowning at her uncertainty, she told herself to put up more resistance. She shook her head in an effort to clear the sensual haze surrounding her. Where was her strong will? Around Walker, it seemed to fade into acquiescence, into a need to please. "It *is* making Geoff happy," she allowed. "Although I don't like bartering for, er, favors. It doesn't feel right."

"But it will feel right, darlin'," he whispered, a wealth of promise in his tone, calling up images of their passionate embrace of the week before. He'd already started to close in when she caught her breath and took three quick steps backward.

"Not—not here." Her hair swung wildly against her cheek as she pivoted to point out the various guests and their children gathering for the afternoon ride. "Not now."

"When?"

"Next week?" she hazarded a guess. He shook his head, and she bit her lip. "Okay. Tomorrow will be fine."

"Tonight." He turned away, waving to the guests, his long strides carrying him quickly over the rough ground.

By dinnertime Stacey was a nervous wreck; she felt like a jackrabbit ready to bolt from a hungry wolf.

Every chance he got, Walker sent her a wicked grin. When she was lifting the cake from the oven, he slid his knuckles down her spine, causing her to nearly drop the pan. Once, while she was at the corrals, watching Geoff curry a horse, Walker came up behind her and whispered in her ear, "Tonight." His breath stirred a loose tendril of her hair, eliciting a shiver from deep within.

She turned and swatted him away, unable to repress the amused tilt at the corner of her mouth that revealed her chagrin and reluctant humor. The truth was, she liked this little-seen, lighthearted side of Walker. She didn't mind his teasing or innuendo, and if her promise to kiss him was responsible for his change in mood, so be it.

With these thoughts firmly in her mind, she felt calmer, more able to handle Walker. She strictly refused entry of other, more disturbing possibilities. Yes, Walker did have a sort of... power to lull her, she supposed. But she would be on her guard, and after one simple kiss, she would wish him a good-night and be on her way.

Now that all this was decided, she could not understand why her heart beat so erratically when he said little during the evening meal, devoting himself to catching her eye, sending sensual messages that threatened and promised everything but a polite embrace.

With a start, she realized Geoff had asked her a question, and she forced herself to turn in her chair and listen. "I'm sorry, what did you say, Geoff?"

"I said, tomorrow Walker's gonna show me how to rope." He sat, half slumping in his chair, his eyelids drooping with exhaustion. Stacey saw that he'd hardly eaten anything.

"Eat, boy," Jim urged, chewing a mouthful of buttered mashed potatoes.

Her eyes went to Walker, who was already pinning her with an expectant, slowly heating stare. She said, "Yes, Geoff, eat a little more." She had to put her mind to the subject at hand. She yanked her gaze away from Walker's. "Roping, huh? Like how the cowboys capture cows?"

"Yep." Geoff held his fork loosely in his right hand, covering his mouth with his left as he tried to hide a yawn. "But first we're starting with a big ole cow skull stuck on a bale of hay. Then—" his nostrils flared as he yawned again "—we go to fence posts and when I get really good, a dog."

She smiled, glancing across at Walker. "Dog roping?"

The sensual light in Walker's eyes seemed to intensify as his gaze roamed her features. "Sure. I figure to teach you a few things, too, Stace."

If she had been on her guard before, now her apprehension doubled. "Teach me? But I don't want to rope a dog."

"Not roping." He waved a hand over his plate of chicken. "Horseback riding. You could use a few pointers. I can help you. Come on out tomorrow. Early. It'll be just you and me. Alone."

They'd be alone tonight, she thought, feeling like the rabbit she'd imagined herself, trapped squarely under the paw of the wolf. Seeing the determination, the hunger smoldering in his eyes, she caught her breath and began to realize just exactly what she'd promised him.

Foolish woman, she berated herself. What had she gotten herself into?

Her brows coming together, she stared at her half-eaten chicken leg and let the guests' conversation and Jim's loud voice swirl around her. Suddenly she knew that Walker had planned no simple kiss, no impersonal embrace, as she'd led herself to believe. If she interpreted the message in his eyes correctly, he was bent on a full-scale seduction!

She had to get out of this.

In his chair beside her, Geoff closed his eyes for a long second. "Geoff," she said more sharply than she'd meant, "you're dead tired and it's only seven o'clock." Putting a hand to his forehead, she assured herself he wasn't running a fever. "You're not getting sick, are you?"

"No, Mom. And I'm not tired." He tried to sit up in his chair, but almost immediately slumped again.

Jim chuckled. "Ranch life isn't so easy, is it, son?"

"I'm not tired," the boy insisted, and even Walker laughed.

Stacey frowned again. "I know you raked leaves today, I saw you with the other boys. Then you went on a trail ride for a few hours. What else did you do?"

"Gave six of the horses baths," he said. "Then Billy and Ted and I tried to catch some fish in the little stream in the horse pasture, but we couldn't get any."

"What about the tack you helped me clean?" Walker asked.

"Oh, yeah." Geoff smiled wearily. "We got this stuff called foot's neat oil—"

"Neat's-foot oil," Walker corrected.

"Yeah. That stuff. And we cleaned saddles."

"Goodness," Stacey said. "No wonder you're all had out." She turned to Walker. "I think he's being overloaded. From now on I want him doing less, all right?"

To her surprise, Walker shook off her concern. "Geoff's fine, he's just sleepy from a good days' work. You coddle him too much."

"I do not—"

"Walker's right." Jim finished off his chicken and, noticing Stacey wasn't eating hers, filched the leg off her plate. "You mollycoddle that boy any more, why, we'll have to put a dress on him."

Lips firmed, Stacey wiped her mouth and tried to hold her temper. "That's a very male-chauvinist thing to say, Jim."

"I'm not wearing any dress!" Geoff said, coming alive.

"A'course not, son." Jim leaned across and lightly boxed the boy's ears. "I was just kiddin'. You're a ranch hand now, aren't ya? That's man's work."

"I'm a junior wrangler," Geoff said.

"That's fine and good," Stacey put in, still determined to have her say. "But I don't want Geoff overdoing it. He's only ten!"

Walker and Jim both continued to argue with her, so they all left the table with the discussion at a stalemate. Tight-lipped, Stacey supervised the cleanup, while the guests sought quiet diversions in the lounge or in their rooms.

Putting Geoff to bed amid his protests, she stayed in the room folding laundry and straightening up. He fell asleep within minutes. She wandered about the room. She was not avoiding Walker.

When she discovered herself primping in front of the mirror as if she were going on a date, she became exasperated. At last she ventured out. Most of the guests had retired, many of them as exhausted as Geoff from the unaccustomed business of horseback riding. She wandered into the kitchen, realizing she'd forgotten to serve the carrot cake. Taking her apron from its hook, she tied it around her neck and waist and walked across the room.

The pan had been placed on a cutting board, and a good half of the cake was gone. She let out a breath, deciding

Rudy must have served it, and made a mental note to thank him tomorrow.

"Hungry?" a low, masculine voice asked.

Stacey whirled. Walker lounged there, one hip against the doorjamb. He straightened and came toward her. "I didn't have any cake, either. I was waiting for you."

"I see." Her hand flattened uneasily at the base of her throat, then smoothed down the front of her apron. Walker watched the path of her palm with great interest.

He was here to collect his debt.

Stacey swallowed with difficulty, anxiety and anticipation warring within her until she felt almost sick. Quickly she turned her back to him and for something to do, she began cutting two squares of the cake and then put them on china plates. She got forks from the drawer, poured mugs of rich coffee, then took a deep breath.

"If you'll open the door, we can sit at the dining table." She held the plates in her hands.

He shook his head. "Naw. It's cozy in here." He took a chair at the small wooden table, this time not straddling it, but sitting properly. "Uh, listen. If you want, we'll go easier on Geoff. He was pretty tired tonight."

"Okay. Thank you."

She served him, going back for their coffee, then again for cream and sugar. While she worked, he said nothing, seeming to enjoy following her movements with his eyes. For a few dreamlike seconds she almost felt like a wife, quietly serving her adoring husband.

At the table she peeked at him over the rim of her steaming mug and decided "adoring" wasn't quite the correct word. Perhaps "lustful" would be closer to the mark. Her chair was a foot away from his, but she felt almost as if she were in his lap. He studied her with shameless interest, raking his gaze down, then inch by inch back up her figure, pausing at every hill and valley. Stacey shifted in her chair, restless, awkward. Was there any way to move her chair away another foot?

"Cake's good," he grunted, taking man-sized bites. "I like the frosting. Never had it before."

"It's made with cream cheese," she explained. When he hunted for crumbs, she raised her brows. "I can't believe you've eaten that whole piece already! Do you want some more?"

"Sure. Will you split yours with me?" He nudged her full plate with his finger.

She looked down; she hadn't taken a single bite. There was still half of the cake left on the cutting board, but she really wasn't in the mood for sweets and figured he might as well have part of hers. With her fork she started to cut her piece in half, but he stopped her with a hand on her wrist.

"You haven't had any yet." He took her fork and held a piece to her mouth, his eyes filled with lazy sensuality.

"Walker, no." Where would this lead, she wondered, such an intimate service from a man to a woman? He'd probably end up by trying to lick the frosting from her lips. That idea conjured up all sorts of other intimate contact.

"Come on, open up," he wheedled. "Take a little. When we kiss, we'll taste the same flavor."

She flushed and folded her hands in her lap. "Walker, stop teasing. Why don't you just kiss me and get it over with?"

When his gaze dropped to her lips and he leaned toward her, she was certain he would heed her advice, but after a moment he relaxed and sat back in his chair. "No. Maybe our kissin' is something you want to be done with, but not me. I want to taste you good, Stace. I want to feel you full against me. I want to hear you whisper my name like you did in the meadow. I've been dreamin' of it."

Walker watched first shock, then wariness and then what could be desire, cross her expressive features. His spirit soared. She was a careful woman—and proud—not one to give herself casually. But he meant to beat down her defenses, tease her, as she'd said, and he felt not a whit of guilt about his intentions. He wanted her. There was no reason on earth why he shouldn't have her.

Startling her, he got up, scraping his chair on the floor. "Let's go into the living room, sit by the fire." When she hesitated, he put a hand under her elbow and urged her to her feet, then held open the swinging door for her to pass through. She wore a dazed expression, like some kind of sacrificial animal being thrown to a lion. He chuckled inwardly, feeling his gut tighten in growing need. *Tonight.*

In the living room they were alone, and casting a quick peek into the lounge, Walker discovered that all of the guests had left for their rooms. Even Jim had gone to bed. Lately, the old man hadn't seemed as robust as he always had, Walker reflected. He'd been paler, too.

Walker shook off the notion. The old he-bear would probably outlive them all.

Kneeling on the hearth of the stone fireplace, Walker stoked the coals with a poker, then laid a big log on top. The dry wood flamed and soon it was blazing. When he turned, he saw that Stacey had taken a defensive posture, standing behind the sofa, the fingers of one hand nervously picking at the upholstery, the other hand rubbing the back of her neck. She still wore the apron over her jeans and plaid, ruffled blouse she'd worn the first day he'd met her. Her hair, cut to fall just below her jawline, gleamed in the firelight, looking like shiny melted chocolate. The blue eyes he'd long admired were wide this evening; he never tired of looking into them.

"Come here." His command sounded husky and forceful, but there was no help for it. These weeks of living so close to Stacey, hoping to catch her smile and often doing so, admiring her smooth legs, small waist and generous breasts . . . it was all catching up with him tonight.

She started for him, then paused. "Walker—" she cast a glance over her shoulder toward the doorway leading to her room, as if she wanted to escape there "—maybe this isn't such a good idea. Maybe—"

"Stacey, come here." He forced the hand resting on his thigh to release the tense fist it had curled into. If Stacey didn't allow him to touch her tonight, he didn't know what he'd do. Go crazy, maybe. Speaking more softly, he urged, "Please. Sit here with me, honey."

She complied, gratifying him. She dropped to the floor before the fire, folding her legs beneath her.

"Fire feels good, huh?"

"Yes." She smiled. "But it's summer. Do you have these evening fires all year around?"

"When it's cold at night." He couldn't seem to take his gaze off her face. She was so pretty, so soft. Just looking at her fired his blood. That and knowing she had at least agreed to let him kiss her. He had to fight the impulse to drag her beneath him on the carpet right now.

Instead, he forced himself to breathe deeply, regularly. He broached a topic sure to interest her. "Geoff's making some friends his own age, playing around the place just like I did, growing up. I think he really likes it here."

She rolled her eyes. "Likes it here? He *loves* it here. And I..." She studied a suddenly fascinating fingernail. "I kind of like it, too."

"Good."

She chanced a look at his face. "I thought you didn't want us here, Walker. You made it plain you hoped I'd leave as soon as possible."

He shrugged. "Geoff's an okay kid. And you're a good cook."

"Chef," she mumbled. The idle gaze she slowly cast around the room, looking at nothing in particular, suddenly seemed forlorn. What had he said wrong?

"Anyway," he tried, "I guess it's all right with me if you stay on a while longer."

"A while? Is that all?" Her forlorn expression intensified.

"Sure." Groping to say the right thing, he added, "Maybe weeks or months longer."

She nodded without enthusiasm. "Weeks or months. I see."

Walker frowned, struggling with her puzzling mood shift. He didn't know what to say to a woman. Didn't have much use for sweet-talking them. The only language he truly understood was tactile.

So he reached out and did the only thing he knew how; he pulled her onto his lap and kissed her.

In his arms she was stiff, clearly surprised by his sudden move, but he persisted, moving his mouth over hers with all the determination of a man bent on persuading his woman to respond. His palms stroked her back soothingly, just as if she were one of his mares. Lifting his mouth an inch over hers, he crooned her name, praised her, whispered dark, hungry words of his passion for her. With small nips, he bit gently at her lips.

When at last she grew pliant, he shifted them off the stone hearth and settled on the thick carpeting. Supporting his back against a heavy chair, he drew her more fully across his lap.

When he lowered his mouth this time, he had passed the point of gentlemanly consideration. His lips seared hers, causing such rising heat that he felt desire boil in his gut like hot coal. Elevating his need for her another notch, she sank her fingers into his hair. She held his head so that their mouths met squarely, with a feminine strength that thrilled him.

Distracting him, her breasts nestled against his chest. He could feel her nipples tighten even through her blouse and apron.

This was Stacey... Stacey, the beautiful woman who'd captured his mind, who'd lived in his consciousness, even when he wasn't with her. Never in his dreams had he dared imagine she would come alive in his arms.

He didn't understand his feelings or his mixed emotions about her. Right now, he couldn't even try. All he knew was that this one particular woman had gotten to him as no other had.

Impatient, he yanked at the strings behind her neck and at her waist and pulled off the apron. Then he drew her blouse from her jeans and thrust his hands beneath to feel the warm skin of her back. He explored each notch of her slim spine until his fingers met the back of her bra. He groaned at the barrier.

Still kissing her, he cupped one palm around her full breast, and with his thumb abraded her responsive nipple. She moaned, her legs shifting restlessly, and he grinned in triumph against her lips. She was answering him, caress for caress! She needed him physically, at least, just as much as he needed her. Sexual energy raced through his veins, roaring in his ears.

He had the buttons of her prim, ruffled blouse half unbuttoned before she imprisoned his hand in hers. "Whoa, cowboy." Her voice was breathy and whispery soft. "Slow down, huh? I...I'm sorry. I never meant for us to go so far."

Staring at her, it took several long seconds for him to surface in the ocean of desire and recognize her good sense. Of course they couldn't make love here. Anyone might walk in. They'd have to go to his room.

There was no time to wonder why he'd never felt so strongly about a woman before. No time to question this fundamental need to make her a part of himself. Driving him was the overwhelming urge to fill her senses, fill her vision and her imagination. He wanted to brand her with his body and, more importantly, burn his imprint upon her mind so firmly that she simply wouldn't see other men.

In one determined motion he set her aside, got to his feet and dragged her up. With her wrist manacled by his hand, he towed her toward the long hall.

"Hold it!" She tugged against his grip. "Walker, stop! Where are you going?"

"To my room. Or one of the spare guest rooms, if you like. It doesn't matter." He couldn't wait to get the rest of her clothes off and discover what he'd fantasized about. He already had her halfway down the hall.

"No! I'm not going there with you. Walker, do you hear me?" She was pulling away in earnest now. "Walker, if you don't stop, I'll scream the house down."

At last her protests got through to him. He stopped dead. "What?"

He abruptly let go of her arm, and she stood before him, rubbing her wrist. "I agreed," she began, then appeared to run out of air. Clearing her throat, she met his gaze steadily. "I agreed to kiss you, nothing else. I don't know how you got the idea I'd allow more."

Propping his fists upon his hips, he scowled ferociously. "You don't, huh? That wasn't you, teasing me this afternoon, stroking my arm, asking favors for your boy, smiling at me, flouncing around like a mare in season?"

She pinkened. "I did not flounce."

"That wasn't you, going all soft when I held you, kissing me back so's any man would think you wanted him?"

She pivoted toward the fire, presenting him with her profile. Her blouse draped out of her jeans where he'd freed it. Her fingers fumbled at the buttons over her breasts. "I—I admit I did kiss you back. As you'll recall, we made a deal for it. But—" she faced him again, entreaty in her tone "—Walker, I can't just casually sleep with you, don't you see?"

"No."

She bit her lip. "There's no commitment between us. Nothing planned."

"What are you talking about?" He clenched his jaw as he worked to rein in his temper. The sight of her blouse, primly redone to the top buttonhole, did him no good at all. He wanted to get her off alone—willing and warm—dammit. Her neatly refastened clothing shouted at him that this wasn't going to happen anytime soon. "Look—" with an effort he sucked in a controlling breath "—you're gonna have interest in this place whether you live here or not. So why not take advantage of the situation? You and I can get along pretty good if we try. You can't deny we want each other. Where's the harm in letting nature take its course?"

The woman was blinking rapidly now, the firelight flickering on her face, her features tense. "A business deal?" she asked tonelessly. "Is that what you have in mind between the two of us? Our sleeping together is part of...business?"

"No!" He stared at her. "Well, yes. In a manner of speaking. What's wrong with that?"

Chapter Eight

"**Y**ou ready?" Walker asked the following morning as Stacey was fixing breakfast. He stuck his head through the kitchen doorway, looking wide-awake, with clean-shaven cheeks and wearing a fresh, blue chambray work shirt. His hat rode on the back of his head.

"Ready for what?" She couldn't help the suspicion in her voice. Last night she'd left him in the living room and retired to a restless sleep. If he expected another kiss, he would have to think again. After his casual assumption that she would sleep with him as if it were a business decision, she could hardly bear to speak to him.

"For your riding lesson. Remember?"

"I don't think I want a...riding lesson from you, Walker." Not with his attitude. She sniffed, mixing flour and brown sugar for coffee cake.

Behind her he was silent. That alone surprised her—she'd expected a hot rejoinder to her casual refusal. Or at least a demand for an explanation. Darting a glance at him, she saw that he stood very still in the half-opened doorway.

He'd angled his face away so that his hat shielded his expression from her once again.

Her irritation with him decreased. She raised a floury hand, almost reaching out to touch him, when the scene from the hallway last night popped into her mind. He'd said, "You can't deny we want each other. What's the harm in letting nature take its course?"

No, she wouldn't succumb to the urge to comfort him again. This time she wouldn't give in. She wouldn't allow herself to be used. If he was hurting, that was just tough. Walker was a grown man, he could take care of himself.

Moving quickly, she bent her mind to measuring cinnamon and nutmeg. Without looking at him, she worked, knowing he was watching her. It made her nervous, made her movements jerky, but she did not turn. She didn't want to know if his eyes would look wounded or merely lustful. At that moment, she didn't want to know the truth. She sensed his departure from the room.

Minutes later, the shrill, high-pitched wail of a young boy penetrated the kitchen window and reached Stacey's ears, even over the sound of the sink's running water. Taking time only to snatch a towel to dry her hands, she ran through the dining room and burst into the early morning sunshine.

From the front steps she could see into the first corral. A saddled horse was trotting loose. Some yards away, a crumpled form lay on the ground, sobbing. Geoff!

Stacey hurled herself forward, running to squeeze between the bars and kneel, panting at the boy's side. "Geoff! My God, are you hurt?"

Racking sobs shook the boy's small frame as he brought his knees up into the fetal position. He tried to speak, failed, and lapsed into frenzied weeping again. "Geoff," Stacey murmured, running shaking hands over him to check for broken bones. She found none, but that didn't mean he wasn't injured internally!

"That's enough." A harsh masculine voice cracked like a whip overhead, and Stacey started, then peered up, squinting into the bright sunlight. A shadow moved over her face. It was Walker, wearing his hat. He bent down, closed his strong hand around Geoff's upper arm and hauled the boy to his feet. "Come on. Stop your crying now. We all take a spill occasionally."

Geoff stood half bent in the center of the corral, tears streaming down his dirty cheeks, a pitiful sight. He tried again to speak, getting out only stuttered hiccups. Rising slowly, Stacey supported her son with both arms. She glared at Walker, hardly believing his attitude. "Geoff could be injured," she told him, her voice quavering. "What do you think you're doing, manhandling him like that?"

Before she could react, the wrangler pulled Geoff away from her and carried him to the horse, who, made curious by all the commotion, had ambled toward them. Walker's jaw was grimly set, suggesting he would brook no argument. He was probably angry with her for refusing him her bed. Too bad, she thought.

He hefted the boy into the saddle. Geoff clutched the horn, intensifying his wailing. "No! No, I can't do it!"

Stacey elbowed by Walker and lifted her arms to Geoff, who eagerly reached down to her. Before she could even touch him, Walker wedged his body between mother and son, brushing Stacey aside. "Excuse me," he said, sounding unapologetic. "Geoff's riding lesson isn't over. If you want to watch, go sit on the rails."

"Mom!" Geoff cried.

"Walker, get out of my way." Stacey gritted her teeth and was amazed when Walker behaved as though he hadn't heard her. He was acting as though he had a right to overrule her decisions!

He collected the reins, pushed them into Geoff's hands and then turned back to Stacey. Taking her arm, he quite forcefully guided her to the rails, circled her waist with his hands and hoisted her onto the top amid protests from both her and Geoff.

"How dare you!" she shouted, incensed. "You are not Geoff's parent. You have no say over his life. Get this straight, Walker Marshall. I am his mother and I don't want—"

"Hush," Walker said. He climbed up beside her and said, "Geoff, now start your horse at a walk. This time, keep a hold of him and make sure he stays on the bit."

The boy made no move at all, he just cried harder.

Stacey bit her lip and felt like crying herself. She realized he probably had no internal injuries—broken ribs would hurt too much to let him wail like that—and certainly his lungs were fit.

But it killed her to see him like this. Geoff had obviously fallen off the horse—he'd failed at something important to him—and the accident had robbed him of all the self-confidence he'd earned since they'd come to the ranch. He'd regressed to the weak little boy he'd been.

Tears did fill her eyes then. Would nothing help her son? Was the outward growth he'd exhibited this summer merely masking inner problems? Her mind was made up: she would take him to a psychologist. Geoff needed counseling. She would put it off no longer.

"Quit bellyaching," she heard Walker callously say to Geoff, and she turned to glower at the man. If she'd thought for one second that he'd allow her to jump off the rails, she would have. But she knew better.

He ignored her again. "Now do as I say. Take a hold of his mouth and cluck to him. Show him who's boss, but don't bully him."

"I don't wanna—" Geoff began.

"A good rider," Walker went on smoothly from his perch beside Stacey, "knows how to convince a horse that the rider's way is the best way. Then he'll *want* to do as you tell him. That's how we get them to trust us. Now squeeze him up into the bridle. There you go.''

Stacey swung back to her son, seeing that he was doing as Walker instructed. The boy's sobbing abated.

Walker lowered his voice, but kept it loud enough for Geoff to hear. "Scotty and Billy will be along soon—I'll be giving them lessons, too.''

The boy glanced around; his crying all but stopped. Just as Walker had intended, Stacey thought waspishly. Naturally, the possibility of Geoff's friends appearing on the scene to catch him crying like a baby would be enough to make him quit.

For several minutes more she watched as Walker continued the lesson. She grew amazed as Geoff first responded to the adult command in Walker's tone, then gradually quit sniffling, and finally sat up in the saddle, looking almost as if he were enjoying himself.

Her anger with Walker faded, cooling to a general irritation. "You got him over his crying,'' she admitted grudgingly, "but I don't see why you found it necessary to browbeat him. He's just a boy, little more than a baby.''

Walker didn't turn to face her. "A ten-year-old boy isn't a baby.'' He kept his eyes on the boy in the corral, who was now passing them at a slow, collected canter. Though the tears were still drying on Geoff's face, she saw the beginnings of a happy grin. He had regained his confidence and was again the cheerful boy he'd become.

"How's he gonna grow into a man,'' Walker asked her in a reasonable tone, "if you keep running interference for him?''

She didn't answer.

Walker didn't take the hint, but went right ahead. "Every time you get on a horse, you gotta realize there's a chance you might make what we call a flying dismount.''

"Cute." She grimaced. But his use of the word "you" distracted her. Was he talking about her? "When I ride with the group, we just walk. I'm not in any danger, am I?"

He shrugged. "I wouldn't say danger, exactly."

"What about the great horseman, Walker Marshall?" she challenged. "I don't suppose *you* ever expect to fall off."

"Happens to me, too." His smile was faint. "But not real often."

She didn't reply to his arrogant remark, choosing instead to hunch one shoulder away from him and concentrate on her son. The boy was smiling now, ear to dirty ear, plainly thrilled to be on horseback, his fall all but forgotten.

Had she coddled him too much?

Maybe, she decided slowly, he didn't need immediate psychological counseling, after all. She would table the idea for a while longer.

Stacey cooked, served meals and spent time with Geoff. Three days passed, during which she tried to ignore Walker, tried not to notice the flex and pull of his shoulder muscles as they moved beneath his shirt. When she'd see him rake his hand through his hair, she tried not to remember how silky it felt, tangled in her fingers. Even his scent, the masculine blending of horse, leather and warm summer breezes unwillingly reminded her of their embrace in the meadow.

Nor did she want to see his frustrated frown whenever he studied her, or the angry, sexual gleam in his hazel eyes.

Although she knew what was in his mind now—all he wanted was her body—the knowledge wasn't enough to kill her physical response to him. This lack of control over her innermost sensibilities ate at her, infuriated her. Consequently she was stiff around him, uncomfortable, resenting the fact that he could make her feel things she had no business feeling, didn't want, couldn't indulge in.

If it hadn't been for Geoff's progress and joy in everyday ranch life, she might have considered packing up and heading back to Los Angeles.

She hadn't given herself to Walker, she reminded herself with a renewal of determination. But she was honest enough to admit she'd wanted to. Recklessly. Wantonly. Desperately.

It wasn't like her at all.

She couldn't trust her own emotions, and she trusted his even less. He'd proven to her, three nights ago as they'd lain before the fire in a passionate embrace, that although he might want her physically, he wanted her to yield to him even more. For business reasons, of course.

Her son was only ten. It would be eleven more years before he could legally begin administering his share of the ranch—supposing Jim died before that time. Stacey sighed, and from the fruit basket before her, collected six huge, green apples she'd been saving to use for pies. Hopefully Jim would live another twenty years. She'd come to appreciate his gruff affection, and he was wonderful with Geoff.

Deciding to go to her room and freshen up before starting on dinner, she hung her apron on its peg. It was only three o'clock, so there was plenty of time to splash water onto her face and brush her hair before beginning the apple pies that she planned to go with her chicken and dumpling dinner.

She'd left the apples on the counter and pushed through the swinging doors when Walker appeared before her.

"We need to talk." He made it a statement, with no room for opinion or argument.

She bristled. "There's nothing to say."

He was tall and dark, standing in her path, his hat cocked over one eye. Intimidating and compelling. Looking at him made her think of long, luxurious kisses that made one tremble.

"I've given you three days to get over your mad, Stace. That's long enough. I'm tired of being ignored."

Not daring to look into his eyes and be seduced by his dangerous brand of charm, she settled her gaze on a bleached cow skull that stood on an end table beyond his left shoulder. Drawing a difficult breath, she told him, "Walker, I think you and I understand each other, don't we? You're interested in quick sex—"

"No. Not quick."

She winced. "All right. Long, slow sex with a willing, convenient woman. Well, I may be convenient, but I'm not willing. I've never been the type to hop from bed to bed. I won't start now."

He lifted one straight black brow. "You want forever?"

The breath she took now trembled in her chest. It was a great risk to admit it. "Yes. I suppose I do."

"What's the problem then? You're here to stay, aren't you?"

"I haven't made that decision yet."

"But if you decide to stay," he pressed, "doesn't that mean you and I will pretty much be living together?"

She gaped at him. "You expect me to live here, sneaking from your bedroom to mine?"

He shrugged, supremely unconcerned. "Why sneak?"

"I have an impressionable child." Shaking with hurt, she thrust her hands into the pockets of her jeans. Had she been crazy, imagining this callous man to be vulnerable? "I won't just live with you as a lover. You think I'll fall into bed with you?"

"I wouldn't put it quite that way."

"No?" She bit the word out. "Would you pretty it up? Couch it in terms to salve your ego—maybe mollify me? Well, it won't work." Before he could reply, she stalked past him, headed for her room. In another minute she wouldn't be responsible for her actions. Never in her life had she struck anyone, but her fury was so intense that right now she wanted to hit him.

The violence of her thoughts impelled her to the door, slamming and locking it behind her. Leaning back against the solid wood, Stacey closed her eyes and willed her racing heart to slow. She'd made mistakes in her life, some doozers. But her failure to recognize that Walker was unable to truly care for a woman was the most unforgivable. And it hurt her more than she could ever have imagined.

In her small bathroom she wet a washcloth, ran it over her face and pressed it to her overheated forehead. The mirror reflected her sorrowful expression. Weary, she turned away.

She forced herself to straighten her shoulders and leave the bedroom. From the hallway she could see Geoff on his way out, closing the front door behind him. He'd fashioned a sling out of the front of his T-shirt and was holding something—probably an armful of kittens, she supposed without much interest.

In the kitchen she was surprised to find Walker calmly drinking a bottle of cola, looking for all the world as if he were waiting for her. He straightened and was about to say something when her gaze slid to the counter. She frowned, then glanced into the now-empty fruit basket. "Where are the apples? I'm going to make pies."

He followed her gaze. "Uh-oh."

Instantly she remembered Geoff, slipping out the front door with something filling his shirt. Whirling, she ran out, racing straight for the wild-horse corral, where she knew Geoff would be going. Darn him! If she didn't get those apples back, there would be no dessert for the guests tonight—something they'd come to expect. Besides, Geoff had to learn he couldn't just take things from her kitchen without asking! She'd give him a tongue-lashing he wouldn't soon forget!

As she rounded the barn at a pace that could only be described as a gallop, the scene before her made her slow to a trot, then a walk. Fifty yards off, she halted, her annoyance with Geoff disappearing like the sun that was dropping behind the mountain.

Geoff was kneeling beside the corral that confined Ridgefire and his wild mares. The boy's hand extended, offering the proud stallion one of her big, juicy, green apples. He spoke softly, mimicking Walker's soft croon, trying to woo the proud horse.

Inside the corral, the stud stood, facing him, ears flicking back, then forward. But he made no move to cross to get the treat.

Stacey hadn't the heart to interfere. Clearly the horse was neither going to be tempted nor tamed by the boy. But it seemed so important to him. She didn't know why; the horse looked much like any other to her. Yet Geoff clearly felt some affinity for the sorrel. She sighed, resting her weight on one leg. She didn't really have to understand.

Booted feet crunched on the ground behind her. She didn't turn when a warm, masculine hand pressed her shoulder. Walker stood with her, watching Geoff's futile attempts, neither of them saying anything.

Finally he said, "You've heard me talking to him about that horse. I don't know why he keeps trying."

Now Geoff tossed the apple into the corral and toward the stallion. It rolled in the dust to within a few feet of the big hooves, but the horse ignored the fruit. Geoff chose another from the front of his T-shirt and held it out, as he had done before.

"It doesn't matter." Stacey felt sad, wishing the damn beast would just walk over and accept Geoff's offering.

"He won't get anywhere." Walker's voice was low, understanding; his hand caressed her.

"I know. But I suppose trying to make friends with Ridgefire won't hurt Geoff—even if he never comes around. We all need to take emotional chances now and then."

Did Walker stiffen? she wondered fleetingly.

She paused, realizing she should be protesting Walker's touch. She shouldn't have quiet, personal conversations with him anymore.

Yet the afternoon sun on her hair and face felt like it had the evening they'd embraced before the fire. It made her drowsy and unwilling to resist when, standing behind her, Walker gently slipped his arms around her waist and linked his hands over her stomach. He propped his chin beside her temple; she could feel his breath fan her cheek.

She was so tired of the push and pull of emotions Walker engendered in her, so weary of the constant emotional vigil she had to maintain. Melancholy at the sight of her beloved son trying so hard to win the affection of the aloof animal...with the sun warming her skin, the gentle breeze smoothing her hair...with Walker holding her sweetly, like a man would hold a woman with whom he was deeply in love, she couldn't fight anymore.

What harm could there be in enjoying this small pleasure, if only for a few minutes? How could luxuriating in Walker's strong arms further rend her already tattered heart?

Finding no answers, she simply leaned back against his strong chest and sighed, loving this moment of quietness and peace. His hold on her tightened in a reassuring, non-threatening way.

She knew he was looking at the wild mustangs over her head when he said, "You know, they're not the prettiest animals around. Their heads are too big, bodies too squatty—most of 'em are scarred up from fighting."

"Yes." She smiled. Even she could see the mustangs' many flaws.

"But I still feel something every time I see them." His voice lowered. "See how their nostrils are different from Ridgefire's? There's sort of a flap that keeps them half closed. Some say for protection when they're grazing in snow."

"Oh, yes," she replied in wonder. "They do look different."

"And they have one less vertebra in their backs than other horses."

"Why?" She felt the shifting of his shrug against her shoulder blades. How she loved being held close to him like this. She felt she could stand in that one spot all day.

"That I don't know."

"And I was under the impression you knew everything about horses."

His deep chuckle ruffled the hair at her cheek. "Damn near," he said, and she laughed with him.

Before them, Geoff was displaying extraordinary patience, still proffering the apple, still whispering to the aloof stallion.

"You know, honey," Walker began, his voice beside her ear low and husky, "if I could do anything to get that horse to warm up to Geoff, I'd do it."

She tilted her face toward him and offered a soft smile. The scrape of his beard stubble felt good on her cheek. "I know," she whispered.

"Then you know why, don't you?"

"Why... what?"

"Why I'd help Geoff, if I could." With his fingertips he stroked her forearms from her hands to her elbows and back again in a lingering caress. "'Cause I like him, Stace. And I'd do a lot for you."

She closed her eyes. He ran hot, then cold, then hot again so often, she felt confused at every turn. Would she ever be able to predict this man, follow his thought processes?

It was all too much, Stacey thought, as the peace she was feeling began to evaporate. She couldn't tell if he truly meant what he was saying, or if he was still simply trying to seduce her. In an effort to lighten the mood, she opened her eyes and smiled at him. "Would you bring me a big bunch of chrysanthemums then? I like fresh-cut flowers."

"Mums?" He echoed, and she thought she heard a scoff somewhere within his tone. "There's only wildflowers around here." His hold on her relaxed, and something in his voice made her want to step away. She did.

"Sorry." She crossed her arms. "I just meant I like it when someone gives me flowers."

He shrugged and crossed his own arms. "Anyway, I don't give flowers."

"That's okay." Uncomfortable now, she eased away. Her melancholy deepened, and she couldn't look at him. "I'm going to see about dessert for tonight." From somewhere she dredged up a smile. "The guests seem to like sweets after dinner."

He nodded, silent.

"See you later then." Feeling awkward, she swung away. Walker had disappointed her yet again.

In the kitchen just before dinner, Stacey allowed Geoff to help her build chocolate-and-vanilla-pudding parfaits. Actually, "allowed" probably wasn't the correct word. "Forced" might be closer. But he hadn't protested too much—ever since she'd gently reprimanded him for pilfering her apples. After the token protest of, "Aw, Mom," he seemed to actually enjoy layering the puddings and adding a cherry on top for a final touch.

As Stacey set the tray of parfait glasses onto the bottom shelf of the big refrigerator, Geoff started chattering about his day. He skimmed over his fall, mentioned playing with Billy and Scotty, and told her about Walker instructing him in horseshoeing.

"And then Walker said to never stand right behind a horse, 'cause you might get kicked." Geoff licked the bowl of the chocolate pudding, getting some on his chin.

She gave him a small frown. "I hope you're not in danger of being kicked."

"Me? I won't. But Walker told me all about this old guy he knows who got four of his teeth knocked out by a ticked-off horse who didn't like getting shod."

"Geoff!" Aghast, Stacey figured it was the expression of horror in her voice that slowed Geoff down.

"Um, never mind about that," he said quickly. "This pudding sure is good. Mom, you're a great cook."

She couldn't help grinning. "Nice try, but it won't work. I know when somebody's trying to sidetrack me." She ruffled his hair and with her index finger, wiped the pudding off his chin.

"Oh." His returning grin was sheepish.

"Besides, I'm not a cook and you know it."

"You're not? What then?"

"Don't you remember?"

He shook his head, bewildered.

"A chef, okay? A chef."

"Oh, yeah."

"Oh, yeah is right."

"Anyhow, Walker lets me help him, no matter how hard the work is. He's a really good rider, too, Mom. We got some new cows in this morning, and he had to rope one that tried to get away. You should have seen him—"

"Whoa, son." Stacey held up one hand. "Do I detect a hint of hero worship?"

"Hero—what?"

"It means you like that person a lot. You look up to him."

The boy nodded vigorously. "Walker's great. He's really...neat." Jumping off the stool, he said, "I think I'll see what Billy's doing." When she nodded, expecting him to leave, he surprised her. "You know, I miss Dad a lot."

Her brows lifted. Geoff had spoken very little about his father since the funeral. In the beginning she'd tried to get him to, but he'd been so unwilling, so sad, she'd given up, hoping in time he would.

"I guess it's hard, growing up without a father," she murmured.

"Only...Dad didn't do stuff with me, you know? He was always working or something."

Stacey took a deep breath, hating to admit that Dennis hadn't been a better father. "He was...a busy man. But he loved you."

Nodding, Geoff dug his toe into the tile flooring. "Walker plays with me. He really likes me."

"You're a likable kid." She wondered why this sudden mention of Walker was accompanied by Geoff's solemn stare.

"Geoff," she began carefully, "are you trying to tell me something?"

"No." He thrust his hands into his front pockets and kicked at the floor again. "But you like Walker a lot, too, huh?"

She laughed without mirth. *Like him?* She was half in love with the man. "Sure, I like..." Suddenly she frowned, her own thoughts catching up with her. In love with Walker?

The notion was stunning in its simplicity.

Clearing her throat, she finished her sentence because Geoff was eyeing her curiously. "I like Walker," she said, but to her own ears her voice sounded almost as if it had come from someone else. Geoff nodded, then pushed through the swinging doors. Stacey stood before them, staring blindly at the wood grain. In love with Walker?

How could she have been so foolish?

Chapter Nine

The woman was curiously quiet, Walker decided, observing Stacey through the evening meal and again the following morning, while he gave Geoff a riding lesson. Normally Stacey spoke her mind, smiled a lot and participated in discussions. But not now. In the time he'd known her he'd seen her pleased, furious, frustrated and even hurt. But never so fidgety... nervous... unhappy.

"That's good, Geoff," he called out absently to the smiling boy in the corral; he was riding the bay who'd dumped him the day before. "Lots of cowboys post—you can learn it, too."

"Posting's sissyfied." Geoff trotted by, bumping in the saddle.

"No, it's not. Now let's see you try. And get on the right diagonal." Walker stole a glance at Stacey. She sat on the front porch steps, staring sightlessly toward the mountains. A small cat rubbed himself against her leg, trying for her attention. She didn't seem aware of it. Her whole demeanor was distracted, so unlike her. Searching for a possible reason, he could come up with nothing. He knew she'd been upset to learn he'd actually expected her to sleep with him. If she'd been angry, he could've understood it—even if she'd slapped him, he wouldn't have been surprised. But sad?

Anyway, where the hell had she thought things were headed between them? Even now, memories of the softness of her throat beneath his lips and of her plump breast filling his hand swamped his mind and stirred his body.

On the rail, he shifted uncomfortably, and had to tamp down the sensual rush of heat. Damn it, but what else were two adults to do who wanted each other?

"Look, Walker!" Geoff called, posting clumsily, yet proud of the accomplishment.

Walker swung back, realizing he'd been staring at Stacey. She hadn't even been aware of his scrutiny; her head was bowed, and her fingers trailed absently over the back of the calico cat. Stacey's normal spunk was one of the things he liked about her. She was soft and feminine looking, but she had an underlying strength he admired. Unlike some he'd known, she would never back down from a man, but would give as good as she got. In both war and in love.

Still, today something was amiss.

Walker didn't question the force that impelled him to approach her. Setting one booted foot on the bottom step, he braced his elbow on his knee. "Morning."

"Oh, hello." Her smile was forced.

"Something wrong?" It would be best to get her feelings out in the open, he guessed. Get her over her mood. He found he disliked the thought of her being unhappy. He'd do anything to bring a real smile back to her face.

"Wrong?" She glanced up. "Nothing I can't handle, I suppose."

At that moment one of the younger, unmarried cowhands walked by on his way to the barn. In his hands a new rope swung. "Hi, boss," he said to Walker cheerfully.

"Going to stretch out this new lariat between the hitching rail and your truck bumper, okay?"

Walker gave him a curt nod, irritated by the interruption.

"Morning, Ms. Stacey. Sure is a fine day." The man paused and respectfully touched his hat with two fingers. A big grin split his face.

"Yes, Harley. It is a nice day." Her returning smile was warmer than the one she'd given Walker.

He fought to keep from scowling at Harley. For the first time Walker actually looked at him. The cowboy couldn't have been more than twenty-five, clean shaven and probably, from a woman's point of view, passably handsome. His nose was straight and unmarred. Walker frowned. "You'd best be getting to that rope stretching."

"Sure, boss. On my way." He gave the rope in his hands a little shake. As Stacey continued to smile pleasantly at Harley, he appeared reluctant to go.

"Now." Walker glared at him, tempted to grab the cowboy by the scruff of the neck and hustle him away.

At last, noticing Walker's fierce glower, the man blanched. Walker watched him walk all the way back to the barn. Just the notion of Stacey being interested in another male made his teeth grit and his fists itch to smash into the other's face. These yahoos had better learn to keep their distance from her!

Trying to calm himself, Walker swung back to Stacey. "You still mad at me?"

She drew a deep breath that lifted her breasts. "No. Not mad."

"Unhappy then?"

She shrugged.

"Stace, I..." He didn't know how to proceed. Most women he'd known either liked him or they didn't. On that basis they went to bed with him or they didn't. He'd never spent time trying to understand one before. It hadn't seemed important to divine feminine thoughts—understand them—learn about them.

But Stacey was different. Walker found himself interested in her opinions and concerned by her moods. She intrigued him. For the first time in his life, he cared about a woman's state of mind.

Reaching out, he framed her velvety cheek with his palm.

She flinched, pulling away as if he'd struck her. "Don't," she whispered.

Eyes narrowing, Walker cursed beneath his breath. She didn't trust him—not for a second. That was as clear as the mountain air.

He felt a sinking futility—his old bitterness—the one emotion that had sheltered him, protected him from hurt throughout his loveless life. "You don't want my touch?" he asked roughly.

"It's... not that."

He waited stiffly.

"It's...I guess I don't trust myself around you. I...react to your touch."

Something inside him brightened. He admired her courage in admitting it. "I guess I—well—" He stopped and lifted his hat, ran a hand distractedly through his hair. Lord, he'd rather jump onto the back of a raging bull than speak to her of his tender feelings. "I... know how you feel."

"Things are complicated, Walker." With a pained expression, she looked at him, then raised her head proudly. "You see, I'm not ready to cast off my moral beliefs or what I think is important. But...when you come near me..." she whispered this last "...I tremble. I *do* want you. I know you're aware of it."

"Yes." He stared at her hotly. Blood rushed through his veins and hammered in his ears. She'd said it. No longer did he have to guess at or interpret her feelings. Letting his gaze linger on the sunlight shining off her hair, he knew he wanted her more, right at that moment, than he ever had before. This lethal attraction was consuming him, he thought, light-headed with sudden desire.

She ran her fingers over the cat, still speaking. It took a minute for him to hear her. ". . . at the same time, I think— I'm afraid—the ranch will always come between us."

The ranch. Of course.

How could he have forgotten, even temporarily?

Giving a savage twist to his mouth, he regarded her with such a sudden loss of hope that he wanted to shout at her, shake her. Nothing he'd ever felt had prepared him for this level of disappointment.

She didn't trust him? Well, that was fine—he trusted her not at all. Never in his life had he been vulnerable to anyone. He'd been autonomous. Aloof. Except for this ranch.

And now, maybe, for this woman.

Even with this knowledge, he couldn't allow himself to believe in Stacey, to leave himself open. Only a fool would risk his land, his livelihood and his home to someone who might have ulterior motives for holding him in thrall.

"The ranch comes first in my book, as well. Not you," he told her brutally. He wanted to hurt her, as she'd hurt him. "And, honey, as much as I think we'd burn each other up in bed, don't ever get the idea that I'd choose you over this land."

She winced, her expression stricken, but he continued to pull away, refusing to believe he'd hurt her. She whispered, "I won't."

"Good." With that, he strode back to the corral, told Geoff in brittle tones that the lesson was finished and stalked into the house.

Behind the closed doors of his room he took a turn around its tight confines—a caged animal. He walked from the window to his pine chest without thinking, squatted and opened the bottom drawer. Withdrawing the aged photograph, he straightened, staring at it. Memories washed over him of that long-ago afternoon.

He vividly recalled his tenth birthday. His mother had given him an inexpensive camera and several rolls of film he'd badgered her for, and in his delight, he'd run about the ranch, snapping shots of everyone and everything.

Yet when he'd tried photographing Jim, branding a load of cows, the older man had exploded in anger. Yanking the camera from Walker's young hands, Jim had ruthlessly opened it, exposing the delicate film to harsh sunlight. He'd ripped it out, cursing at Walker, who'd watched dumbly.

"Don't ever take my picture without permission, you hear?" Jim had shouted, his unreasonable fury a complete mystery to the ten-year-old boy. Too frightened to do anything but scoop his camera from the dirt where Jim had flung it, Walker had slunk back to his room, comforted only by the awareness that he'd already finished a roll of film and had it in his pocket.

When the pictures were developed, he didn't show Jim, knowing there was at least one shot of the branding. It was years before Walker had become mature enough to understand the full impact of what he'd seen. In fact, if he hadn't kept the picture, he might not have believed it.

Rustling.

In the years that followed, Jim had worked hard to be a good neighbor to others in the area. He'd generously shared water rights, had looked the other way now and then when poor families in the area "accidentally" butchered a Bar-M steer for their dinner table. He'd participated in community affairs, lent his support, offered sound opinions. Always, he'd worked hard on the ranch.

Walker couldn't take any of that away from him. And Walker knew his stepfather's popularity in these mountains was important to him. He made no bones about deriving great satisfaction from being thought of as a big man in the community.

That was why the rustling was so hard to believe.

Walker came back to the present with a jolt. The photo showed a younger Jim, crouched over a calf that lay in the dirt. Jim held a red-hot iron with the Bar-M brand. He was about to burn it onto the calf's flank—over a brand that read Running W. Old Walt Winter still owned the Running W spread over the mountain, a prosperous rancher, who might not have noticed the small but systematic loss of cattle.

Walker crossed the room and shoved the incriminating photo back into the drawer. As soon as he'd grown old enough, he'd done some checking and determined that Jim's rustling had stopped years before. The old man had quit the risky practice after he'd taken enough to support the Bar M during that one critical year. At least there was that.

Still, there were a few of those calves, now gnarly old cows, still alive and in a far pasture, Walker knew. He only had to slaughter one, and the inside of the hide would give proof of the burned-over brand, something that was not visible from the hair side.

If that wasn't enough for a criminal prosecution, the photo, together with the hide, would irrefutably prove that Jim had used underhanded means to keep the ranch afloat. Walker smiled grimly to himself, not a shred of humor in him. Jim would never allow that information to get out.

Uttering a rough sigh, Walker sank onto his bed and stared sightlessly at the wood-paneled wall. All these years he'd held the power to destroy Jim, bring the big man to his knees.

But he hadn't done it. Even with the acrimony between them, there had never seemed to be a good enough reason to ruin a man's life for his past mistakes. The why of Jim's thievery was now clear; the Bar M had been failing, so he'd done the only thing he could to save it. Walker wondered uneasily if he himself were facing the loss of his land—his family heritage—if he could be driven to the same extremes.

Well, the land was threatened now, albeit from a different quarter. By Jim's new will. By Geoff's coming ownership. By Stacey's involvement. Walker didn't know what the future would hold. He was confused and frustrated by his new feelings toward Stacey. Once life had been merely a simple struggle. Now, with such deep distrust between Stacey and himself, he didn't know what to do.

Perhaps it was time to show Jim his evidence. Privately, of course. Not for a minute did he think Jim would allow Walker to go public with it. Walker was as certain as he'd ever been in his life that Jim would capitulate; Walker knew he could force Jim to change his will.

Stacey and her son would be out. He would have no more confusing emotions to deal with. Life could go on as it always had. The distractions of Stacey, with her slim body and sunny smile, would end. There would be no more Geoff, dogging his steps, asking eager questions and getting in the way. Life would be simple again, the way it used to be, the way he wanted it.

Setting his jaw, Walker stared at the wall and reminded himself that he wanted things to return to the way they were before. Definitely.

The time was coming to decide about her future, Stacey told herself sternly. She must choose whether she and Geoff should make their home at the ranch or go back to Los Angeles.

She wasn't about to let Walker run her life. For too many years during her marriage to Dennis, she'd allowed her husband to push her around.

No more.

Yet if she stayed... would she eventually end up in Walker's bed? Each day her attraction to him grew. She hated the idea of becoming nothing but a notch on his bedpost, but the fight she was waging within herself was slowly eroding her defenses.

Stacey shivered, rubbing her arms against the chill in her bedroom. Wasn't Walker the type of man who would have no qualms about doing *anything* to keep his beloved land?

For two days she wrestled with the pros and cons, but by the end of the second, found herself no closer to a solution.

As she got ready for bed that evening, she smiled at her sleeping son, curled under the blankets of his twin bed next to hers. Lately she'd made sure he went to bed a little earlier, and he hadn't been so exhausted by the end of the day. She pulled a floor-length, flannel gown from the drawer, then, hearing the front door open and close, laid the gown across a chair.

It had to be Jim, coming home after a day in town. He'd left again that morning, speeding down the mountain road on his mysterious mission as he'd done several times before. What he did was none of her business. She shrugged, letting herself quietly out of the room. It was time they talked.

She intercepted him on his way to his bedroom. "Jim," she called softly, careful not to wake the guests. The older man paused in the shadows, his meaty hand on his doorknob. His shoulders were hunched tiredly, his face sagging a little.

"Yes?" He didn't remove his hand from the knob.

Summoning her courage, she clasped her hands. He was an intimidating man, and she had some very direct questions to ask. "Can I speak with you? In your office?"

He offered her a weary half smile. "Sure."

After the door had closed behind them, Stacey took her customary chair in front of the desk, and Jim settled behind it with a heavy sigh. "What's on your mind?" he asked without preamble.

"I've been thinking quite a bit about moving here—if Geoff and I should."

He nodded.

"And...I know it sounds foolish, but I can't decide. So..." She rushed on when he seemed about to speak. "I thought I'd best talk with you. You see, I've wanted to ask you this before but—" she grinned nervously "—I didn't have the nerve."

He spread his hands wide. "Ask away."

She cleared her throat. "Yes. Well, I was wondering why you've decided now, of all times, to write your will. I mean, Dennis has been gone for over a year, which isn't long, but it still strikes me as odd. The timing is odd."

His features tightened. "I told you. Geoff's my grandson. My only blood relative. I want to watch him grow."

"Uh-huh," she said, not quite convinced. "What else?"

Ruddy color filled the flesh over his cheekbones, and he averted his eyes. "What do you mean, 'what else?'"

"There's more, isn't there?" Her voice was quiet. "Something you're hiding. Don't you think it's time you told me?"

"Now, girl, I told you. It's just that I want..." His voice trailed off, and his eyes were unable to meet her steady regard. All at once he dropped his forehead onto his palm and heaved his shoulders. "All right. I guess it doesn't matter if you know."

She nodded briefly, strangely tense. She had no idea what he would say next.

"I...I've been under a doctor's care."

She frowned. "Are you sick?"

"In a manner of speakin'." He hesitated. "Heart trouble."

Half coming out of her chair, she gasped. Dennis had died of a sudden stroke. His heart hadn't been strong, and they hadn't even known. It was hereditary, the doctors had said.

"My God, Jim!"

"It's all right." He tersely waved her down again. "They've got me under such close wraps, I can't hardly breathe. I'm taking pills and undergoin' tests and the like.'' He muttered, "A lotta bother, if you ask me."

"No." She shook her head. "It's good the doctor is watching you. If we'd known about Dennis..." She couldn't finish.

"Well, anyway, I found out several months ago. I realized I might not have so much time left. Guess the good Lord wants me to rethink what I want for my final years. And what I want is family. You and Geoff. Living here."

She barely heard him. "That's why you've disappeared to town so many times." She kept her gaze on him. "Walker doesn't know, does he?"

The big man shifted in his chair.

"Why, Jim?" Stacey pressed, scooting closer to the desk. "Why haven't you told him? He's your family, too!"

He studied the suddenly fascinating ceiling. "He and I don't talk much." He smiled without humor. "But then, neither did Dennis and I. Margaret mostly raised Dennis. I didn't like the way he was."

"The way he was?" she repeated, confused.

"Kinda...soft. Liked to stay inside, reading and playing quiet games. He didn't like ranch smells, didn't like animals." He shuffled papers on his desk and his mouth twisted unhappily. "That's not good for a boy. Or a man."

"Walker told me once that Dennis wasn't physical," she said, thinking fast. "And during our marriage he certainly never participated in sports. But there's nothing wrong with that."

"No? Well, I don't know anymore. Guess I shoulda' been more understanding." For the first time Jim looked truly sad, and the sight saddened Stacey.

"Guess I never shoulda' pushed him off the ranch like that."

Her brows lifted at this new shock. She put her hands flat upon the desk. "*You* drove him away? I thought you said it was Walker who did that."

He grimaced. "I've always been a hard man." He lumbered to his feet, walked to the window and stared out into the night. "Back when the boys were eighteen, one day I came into the house after a hard day of riding. There was Dennis, writing letters to colleges, trying to get accepted to one. Now don't get me wrong, college is a fine thing for some. But that day I finally realized Dennis wasn't gonna stay here and continue the work I'd built for him."

"So you threw him out."

He eyed her balefully over his shoulder. "Yes. But I tried to get him back. I paid for his education, sent him money. But he never came home. He didn't want to."

Heartbroken for everything in the past she couldn't change, Stacey knew at last her decision was made. She would stay on the ranch. Jim needed her. Geoff was crazy about it, and she'd made a place for herself there, as well. Lastly, she was in love with Walker. Maybe someday he'd come to care for her. It seemed so obvious now, so clear, that she wondered why she'd had difficulty making up her mind.

But she knew why. Walker.

Getting to her feet, she murmured a good-night to Jim and thanked him for confiding in her. She went to her room and slipped into her nightgown in the dark, not wanting to wake Geoff. Once in her bed, she lay staring at the moonlight on the walls for a long time. Jim had certainly made mistakes in life—one son was gone and the other irredeemably alienated. Yet now he wanted to salvage what he could of his family.

Sighing, she turned onto her side beneath the comforter. This house must have held such emptiness all these years without Margaret's soothing presence! It was becoming increasingly apparent that once Margaret died, Jim had been ill-equipped to deal with two headstrong, twelve-year-old boys, on top of running both a working cattle operation and a guest ranch. It was certainly understandable—that kind of load would bend or break most others. But Jim had survived by toughing it out—by being tough with his son and stepson.

Still... She rolled onto her other side and stared into the darkness. It didn't explain why he'd completely disapproved of both Dennis and Walker. Especially Walker. Jim had admitted why he'd driven his own son away. She'd heard other tales of studious fathers burdened with athletic children. Conversely, of outdoorsy fathers, like Jim, saddled with bookish kids. But the truth was: neither was wrong. Parents and children were simply different. Through love, many parents learned to adapt to and even appreciate the differences in their children.

Jim had not been able to overcome his prejudice toward Dennis. But why not Walker? By all accounts, Walker had been horse crazy, hard working, from the beginning a cowboy in the making. He'd become like Jim and eschewed college to remain on his beloved ranch, just as Jim had wanted Dennis to do.

Walker should have been Jim's dream son.

So why had he been refused Jim's affection?

Stacey had no answer. She wished she'd asked Jim why, when she'd had him talking. It was a personal question, one sure to cause discomfort. But it somehow seemed important to fully understand Walker's childhood.

She would ask Jim in the morning, she decided. She would discover the truth.

Jim appeared to wilt at her question. He still looked tired, although he must have felt better to get up so early. The clock in the kitchen read barely five a.m., long before the guests rose.

She poured him a cup of coffee, making sure it was decaffeinated, and surreptitiously removed the butter from the kitchen table, replacing it with cholesterol-free margarine. Heart trouble meant a change in diet. She'd make sure he ate better. He took a sip of coffee, grimacing at the taste, then slathered margarine onto an oversized blueberry muffin while considering her question.

"Why didn't I treat Walker better?" he echoed as she sat with him, her hands curled around her own mug of coffee.

She nodded. "Wasn't he everything you wanted Dennis to be?"

The big man heaved a sigh. "That's just it, I guess."

"That's it?" She frowned, studying his craggy features. Comprehension dawned slowly. "You mean . . . Walker upstaged Dennis? Walker was able to do all the things you wanted of your own son?"

"Dennis never failed to disappoint me!" Jim flared suddenly. He swallowed the rest of his coffee in big gulps, not seeming to notice that it was still steaming. "I—I wanted to feel pride in him, dammit, pride in my own son!"

"He gave you no joy, Jim? Didn't he have other qualities you could find to appreciate?"

He shrugged. "Dennis was a sneaky little kid. Kinda' cunning."

"And Walker?" Now she was beginning to see the way things had been. "I'll bet he was open. Honest."

Jim shrugged again, looking uncomfortable. "Guess I resented that. Walker seemed to succeed everywhere Dennis didn't."

"Oh, Jim." Stacey felt the poignancy of it all. Sadness and pain for the boys' lives. No wonder Dennis had been a cold man; he'd had a hard teacher.

No wonder Walker knew little of emotional intimacy; he'd never experienced it.

As she looked at the man responsible for their misery, she couldn't even summon any anger toward him. Jim was old now and in failing health. He appeared remorseful. By bringing herself and Geoff to the ranch, he was trying, in his way, to remedy his errors. Dennis was lost to him forever. But Geoff wasn't.

Neither was Walker.

Stacey bundled a protesting Geoff into her car later that
morning, intent on heading down the mountain to Bakersfield for a respite from both Jim and Walker. She didn't really have to take Geoff, but he did need new blue jeans; his
one pair had been taking quite a beating from all the use.
Besides, she wanted his company. They'd had little time
alone since coming to the Bar M.

After purchasing his clothing in a large department store,
she paused in the women's section. A rack of Western-yoked
shirts in a array of colors beckoned. Before she could change
her mind, and to Geoff's delight, she chose three shirts for
herself, then decided to go all the way. She had Geoff help
her select new cowboy boots.

"Mom, you look just like a real cowgirl!" her son enthused, and she felt a flush of ridiculous pleasure spread
over her cheeks.

"Oh, you're crazy." She tousled his head. "Come on,
let's get some ice cream. I'll even spring for your favorite."

"Rocky road?" he said hopefully.

"You bet." They got cones, and Geoff talked, mostly
carrying on about all the exciting ranch activities and his
new friends. She was content to listen, marveling at the
change in him. He was taller, had a healthy tan and was
definitely heavier. His demeanor had altered just as much;
even his posture was more erect, and his manner more confident. He looked people straight in the eye now, laughed
often. Ranch life was doing wonders for him.

She smiled, throwing an arm about him as they crossed
the street and entered the grocery store, so she could stock
up on kitchen supplies. He was still working on the cone,
some of the ice cream rimming his lips. She'd made the right
decision, she told herself, by remaining on the ranch. Even
if the move would only benefit her son. Who knew what

might have happened if she'd forced him back to the city, back to his old school and old insecurities?

"Mom, I'm gonna get some gum balls from the gum machine outside, okay?"

"Don't you think you've had enough sugar for today?"

"No." He smiled and trotted off. She chuckled, liking his high spirits.

Pushing a cart, she headed down the produce aisle. From there she had a clear view of his blond head through the store's front windows as she chose fruit and vegetables.

Suddenly she saw two boys approach Geoff. They were the same troublesome kids who'd visited the ranch the week before—she recognized the redhead and his friend who'd taunted Geoff and Billy. She remembered their parents had said they lived in Bakersfield. Her heart sank.

The two confronted Geoff, standing several feet apart as if facing off for a battle. Just then, a customer walked through the automatic doors, opening them, and Stacey clearly heard the redhead's comments.

"You say you're not a wimp? I say you are!" He punctuated his insolent remark by putting a finger on Geoff's collarbone and pushing him back an inch.

Geoff said nothing; he merely frowned at him. And from her vantage point, Stacey could see three red gum balls clutched in his fist, the dripping ice cream in the other. The doors closed, and she bit her lip, frantically trying to decide what to do. Her hand closed on a cantaloupe in a huge display as she wondered if she ought to interfere.

"Need help, ma'am?" The produce manager, a fortyish, balding man in a white apron eyed her curiously.

"No!" She wanted to tell him to hush; she wanted to catch the rest of the conversation from the other side of the windows.

His gaze dropped to the cantaloupe she was squeezing. "Would you like a ripe melon you can eat today, or perhaps one to save for next week?"

She shook her head, summoning a plastic smile. "Thank you, but I can choose my own." She made a show of squeezing several more, hoping he'd go away.

The other boy's hand flashed out, flicking Geoff's ice-cream cone onto the ground. It oozed onto the concrete in a messy pile. Stacey gasped. Another customer walked in, opening the doors, and she strained again to hear.

"Perhaps," the produce manager suggested, "you'd care to inspect the ones on the other side? They're considerably larger."

She turned on him, stamping her foot in frustration. "Would you leave me alone? I don't like cantaloupe! I never have and I never will!" Peering back out the windows, she barely caught the man's expression of surprise. Both of her hands still rested on the cantaloupes.

Outside, there were two boys against one. And the one was her son! He could get hurt—or worse—be backed into a corner, be humiliated, and lose all the confidence he'd gained!

The other boy had joined in now, reaching out to muss Geoff's hair and laugh. They egged each other on, advancing toward Geoff until his spine was against the store windows.

Enough was enough! Stacey turned her cart and began to march down the aisle with a vengeance, when Walker's words echoed in her mind. "How's he gonna grow into a man if you keep runnin' interference for him?"

Her steps faltered. Walker was right. Geoff had to learn to fight his own battles, even if he got a bloody nose in the process.

Close to the doors now, Stacey saw the redhead stick his nose into Geoff's face and heard him cry, "Wimp, wimp, wimp!" To add insult to injury, he planted one hand in the middle of Geoff's chest and shoved.

Geoff slid along the wall, nearly falling.

Suddenly he came alive. Regaining his balance, he reached out, put his own hands on the other boy's chest and shoved back. The surprised redhead reeled. His friend stepped in, and Geoff shoved him, too—so hard the kid fell ignominiously, landing on the hard concrete with a thump.

"Call me what you want!" Geoff yelled, fists held before him, face red with anger. "I can ride and brand and rope. I do a man's work."

For the first time the two boys eyed Geoff with uncertainty.

He took a step toward the redhead, his chin thrust forward. "Get out of here right now, or I'm gonna rope you and brand your face."

Shocked by Geoff's new confidence, they scrambled back. "Okay, don't get so ticked off," the redhead said. Wary now, he started walking away, his friend hard on his heels.

Still on her side of the windows, Stacey smiled. She'd never been so relieved and proud in her life! She clasped her hands beneath her chin and longed to throw her arms about her son. Never before had he tried to defend himself from bullies; it was something she'd been at a loss to teach him.

Geoff kicked at his fallen ice cream and opened his hand, selecting a gum ball. His face returned to its normal color, and he appeared almost unmoved by what had happened.

It seemed the rough, pragmatic ways of the countryside had rubbed off on him. Stacey sighed. Whether they went back to the city or stayed on the ranch, her son would be fine. And she had to admit that much of Geoff's new confidence had been gained at Walker's side.

Chapter Ten

"Geoff and I are staying. We'll be living here permanently now." Stacey stood tensely before Walker late that same afternoon. The long shadows cast by the mountains were bringing dusk swiftly, and some of the heat was dissipating. She waited for Walker's reaction, her hands held before her, fingers twisted tightly. Even after his harsh words earlier in the day, she was certain he had some feelings for her.

"Staying, huh?" He stood before the watering trough and bent to splash water over his face. "You don't really think I'm surprised, do you? It's what you wanted all along."

His features looked wooden in the fading light, his cynical smile harsh. Stacey studied him, feeling a slow depletion of hope. In spite of their differences, she'd begun to wish for a real future for them.

But now, taking in his contemptuous demeanor, she saw more clearly. She'd naively ignored the signs—all his avowals of mistrust. How very stupid she'd been. But she'd felt so perceptive, overlooking what the man had said and believing instead in his actions.

Walker was a hard, cold man. With plenty of reason. But she'd kept faith, had imagined she could help him change, allow the true generosity in his nature to surface.

How stupid!

Water droplets clung to his jaw, where he hadn't reached with the scrap of towel to wipe them off, and his beard was starting to grow, leaving a dark, masculine shadow over his cheeks. He stood straight and tall and handsome before her, and she knew she'd never loved him more than she did at that moment. Despite his faults, and she believed she knew them all, he was a fine man.

"Walker, I didn't come to steal this place from you." Her voice was high, its tone uneven. She had the most unsettling notion that any chance she had with him was slipping away. Making a supreme effort to remain calm, she asked, "Why do you believe I'm so coldly ambitious?"

"Why?" he barked. Resting one fist on a lean hip, he looked at her coolly. "What have you done to make me disbelieve it? You showed up here for what you said was a two-week stay. I always knew it'd be for good."

"But I didn't," she cried, wanting desperately to get through to him. "How could I know?"

He shrugged, unmoved. With an edge of sarcasm, he said, "Feminine intuition?"

She stared at him helplessly. No convincing words came to mind. Heart-searing pain stabbed through her, leaving her weak and feeling sick. In that second she finally realized that she would never enjoy Walker's love. His lust, perhaps. Careless affection, maybe. But love, never.

Hot, agonizing tears built in her eyes, burning there, banking on her lower lids.

Without saying anything at all, Stacey turned away from the man she loved and walked with dragging steps toward

the house. As she turned, she thought she saw him frown,
put out a staying hand, as if to take back his harsh words.

But she did not pause, no longer able to believe signifi-
cant caring existed in his soul. She must have been mistaken. She'd never had his heart. She never would.

Halfway to the house, an angry shout came from the far
corral, followed by a hoarse cry. Jim's cry. Stacey whirled,
and for an endless second her gaze locked with Walker's.

As one they bolted for the corral.

They found Jim in a small pen adjacent to the wild horses'
corral. Harley and another cowboy stood outside the open
gate. One man held a rope and yelled at the single horse inside. On the ground inside, Jim lay sprawling, leaning on
one elbow. One hand was pressed to his forehead, and Stacey saw he was staunching the flow of blood from a deep
gash. The red stuff seeped through his fingers and dripped
down into the dust. She felt her heart give a fearful leap.

"What's going on?" Walker shouted, sliding to a halt at
the pen.

The cowboy with the rope shook it at the dun-colored
horse that was madly galloping around and around inside
the pen. It wore a halter with a trailing lead rope. "Jim was
working with that crazy yearling. It reared up, kicked Jim
in the head with a front hoof. Now it's gone loco."

Rushing to the rails, Stacey noted that indeed, the horse
was acting wild, circling the pen at breakneck speed. His
hooves dug into the hard-packed earth and sent up dust that
hung in the air.

The panicked horse's eyes were opened wide, the whites
showing. With all the dust, it was hard to see. Stacey choked
and coughed, praying for Jim to get up and walk out.

Jim was about to be trampled!

The two cowboys yelled at the horse. Walker sliced his
hand through the air for silence. Abruptly the men quieted
and Walker started into the pen.

Harley caught at his sleeve. "Are you crazy? Don't go in there, man!"

Shaking him off, Walker reached Jim just as the dun came around again, his nostrils flaring. The thousand-pound animal bucked wildly, wheeled, then raced closer. Behind him, Stacey caught her breath and for a timeless second her heart stopped. "Walker," she whispered.

He ignored her. Moving into a protective position in front of Jim, Walker raised a hand to the animal and waited calmly. The dun escalated into a full gallop and bore down on the two men, but Walker stood stock-still. At the last second, the horse came to a sliding stop five feet away. It snorted and threw up its head, reversed direction and thundered the other way.

Harley and the other cowboy slipped through the rails to help Walker, who had already reached Jim. The older man struggled up, refusing help. Stacey saw Walker stand back stiffly, his eyes pained.

Oh, Jim, she cried inwardly, *let Walker help you for once!*

He did not. The men shut the gate. Stacey met the wounded man and fussed over him. Dirt caked his wound, and it already looked swollen and ugly. But he was conscious.

Glancing over her shoulder, she saw that Walker had not left the pen. Instead, he was speaking soothingly to the horse, murmuring low assurances, walking slowly toward him. The dun snorted again in the settling dust, but slowed to a trot and then stood on the far side. It trembled from head to tail, sides heaving.

Jim was obviously dazed, but he tried to shake off the men helping him. "Let me stand on my own feet, you idiots," he said gruffly, but as soon as they let go, he swayed.

"Take him up to the house," Stacey instructed Harley. A dark bruise was spreading out from the cut.

"Let me go, I tell you," Jim said, staggering again. In spite of his protests, Harley and the other man flanked him, took each of his arms over their shoulders and started for the house.

For a moment Stacey hung back to see what would happen in the corral. At first, the dun shied from Walker, but soon it allowed him to approach. The wrangler held out a hand, offering to let the horse smell him. Carefully it nosed Walker's hand, then Walker closed the distance between them and blew gently into its nostrils. He scratched its ears and ran his hands over the animal's eyes and down its mane. The horse stood, dropping its head, as if relieved to have a sane human in whom to trust.

Even through her own pain, Stacey had to admire Walker's magical skill with the animal. His voice, his touch, his deep understanding, along with something extra, some additional sense, combined to create a unique rapport with horses, something she doubted few could claim.

His touch had created magic within her, as well.

Hurrying into the house after Jim, she made him sit in a kitchen chair, then spent several minutes shooing out the men, along with an anxious Geoff and Billy and half of the guests. After assuring them at least six times Jim would be fine, she closed the door and lifted the clean towel she'd given him to staunch the blood. The bleeding had slowed to a trickle, so she could clearly see that the gash, although two full inches long, was not deep. The bruise underneath from the blow of the hoof would hurt him worse in the long run.

"You'll need to see a doctor," she told him, thinking about his heart as well as the gash.

"I guess," he replied grudgingly. "Call Doc Bailey from over the hill. He'll come."

She called, and in minutes had the doctor's assurance he was on his way.

"Well," she said, standing before Jim, "You're going to have quite a headache."

He looked at her with baleful eyes. "I already do. That damned dun cayuse took a fright when I was handlin' him and reared on me! I don't know—"

"I told you—" Walker's voice came from the doorway "—to let me train him. He's skittish—just a colt—and needs special handling."

Jim turned his glower on Walker, who was helping himself to coffee. "I been horse training since before you were born. When I need your help, I'll ask for it."

Shrugging, Walker sipped at his steaming mug. "I'm better with them."

"Well, you're good," Jim allowed. "But I don't know about better."

Stacey listened to the exchange and shook her head. It was as obvious as the cut on Jim's face that these two men cared for each other. They were just too proud to admit it. There had to be a way to bring the two together. It was a crime for this dissension to continue. She pursed her lips, thinking.

Suddenly she blinked, amazed at the simplicity of her idea. Why not just force them, right now, to tell each other the truth? Walker should know what had been in Jim's mind all these years. He should know why Jim had mistreated him. And Jim should realize he'd been an important father figure to Walker. She had a feeling things would soon come to a head between them, anyway.

Later, if they both ended up hating her for pushing the confrontation, so be it. She would have done her best.

Collecting antiseptic, bandages and gauze from a kitchen cupboard, she said, as casually as she could, "Jim, I wish we could wait for a better time, but before your accident I'd just finished telling Walker that Geoff and I are going to make our home here."

The big man lowered the bloody towel and sat up straight in his chair. "I knew you'd make the right decision."

Walker's eyes flickered.

Stacey caught the small movement and swallowed hard. "Yes. Well, Walker's not too happy about it."

Jim gave Walker a measuring glance. He harrumphed. "He'll get used to it."

Walker stiffened.

"So," Stacey continued forcefully, before a new argument could break out, "I think maybe it's time you explained to him what you told me last night."

His gaze grew wary. "Which part?"

She set her supplies on the table at his elbow, folded her hands and fixed him with a determined stare. "All of it."

He hesitated. From the window the fading light of dusk fell on Jim's shaggy head, bringing highlights of silver from the gray. He studied Stacey. She detected a speculative gleam in his eyes, as if he thought the idea was a good one. Stacey held her breath. Surely he could see how the truth would heal?

Without heat, he muttered, "Don't see what good it'll do."

"Tell me what?" Walker demanded, setting aside his coffee.

"About your childhood," Stacey filled in, quickly cleaning and bandaging Jim's wound. It would do until the doctor arrived. "About why Jim has been, er, gruff with you."

"Gruff?" Walker laughed without mirth. "That's what you call it?"

Stacey nodded at Jim, who sat uneasily in his chair. She knew this would be difficult for him. Maybe even more difficult than she'd guessed. His skin had a grayish cast, and his massive shoulders were hunched.

"Stacey," he said. "It's not a good idea to push this."

"Try, Jim." She nodded at him again, hoping she looked positive.

"I don't know where to start."

Walker's voice cut between them. "At the beginning." He leaned a hip against the doorjamb and crossed his arms.

Jim heaved a sigh, dropped his gaze to the oak flooring and kept it there. "Stacey and I had a heart-to-heart last night. I told her things... things I've never said to anybody before. They were about you."

"Yeah?" Walker cocked his head, arms still crossed, for all the world appearing confident, arrogant. But Stacey, who knew him well now, could see past his cockiness to the uneasy alertness in his eyes.

"When your mama passed away," Jim went on jerkily, "I was left with you two boys. It was a shock, losing Margaret so fast to cancer like that, then having you and Dennis to deal with. While Margaret was alive, I let her handle you. I was busy with the ranch."

"What's all this got to do with anything?"

"Please, Walker," Stacey interjected. "Just listen."

Touching the bandage over his eye as if he didn't know what to do with his hands, Jim went on. "I... well, I got tired pretty fast of tryin' to get Dennis on a horse. He didn't like them."

Walker nodded once. "I remember. So?"

"He also disliked cattle, fence-mending, range care—I couldn't even get him interested in the ranch accounts. It was like—" he paused, holding his palms up "—like he was born to another man."

Stacey darted a glance at Walker, watching for his reaction. He made no move. At least he was listening. She didn't know if she should be pleased or worried.

Jim said, "I was... ashamed." He winced. "Of my own son."

At Walker's gasp of surprise, Jim haltingly explained, "You were the boy I admired. But I couldn't handle it. The fact that it was a boy not of my own blood who gave me pride...well, it rankled."

Walker snorted. "You had some way of showing your pride."

"Instead of praising you, guess I took out my frustration on you. Pretty soon, it just became habit. Anyway, it's partly why I said you and Stacey can't marry. 'Cause it felt...well, like just one more way you'd win over Dennis. You'd get his widow." The big man glanced up finally and met Walker's astonished gaze.

Walker didn't say a word.

"So I want to thank you for helping me today—with that crazy dun. I think the stupid cayuse would've done a tap dance on my head if you hadn't stepped in."

Walker stood stiffly, pale under his deep tan. His jaw was so tense, it looked set in bronze. Even his fists, held tight against his thighs now, were clenched with white-knuckled force.

Filled with compassion, Stacey waited, knowing this was a lot for Walker to absorb at once. Trying not to hover anxiously, she refilled his mug with fresh coffee. He paid no attention.

"No," he said, his tone curiously without inflection. "He wouldn't have hurt you intentionally. And I didn't do much. The horse was scared. I just calmed him down."

"Yeah. Anyway, I don't guess I deserve your help, but...you saved my life. Thanks. It wasn't right, how I treated you as a boy. Truth is, I never felt good about it, but I couldn't seem to change. Now...well, I'm sorry for it." The big man held out his callused paw. "Shake?"

Stunned, Walker stared at the outstretched hand as if it were a three-headed monster. Slowly his eyes rose to meet Jim's. "You...you want to shake?"

"Sure."

Walker swung to Stacey, gauging her reaction. After several charged seconds he turned a shoulder toward her, as if unable to bear the deep compassion she knew must be in her expression. Suddenly he threw back his head and started laughing. The laughter echoed in the room, and Stacey glanced uncertainly at Jim, wondering what to do. Jim frowned.

Eventually Walker stopped, his laughter fading into chuckles. "That's prizewinning, Jim. I'm impressed. Even for you, that's got to take guts." His smile chilled into a cold, frightening thing. "To expect my forgiveness after all these years you've made my life a living hell. Yep, guts."

"Walker..." Stacey began. This wasn't what she had in mind.

"And now," he went on, clearly not hearing her, "you want to shake hands—like how a mama kisses a baby's scratch all better?" He guffawed incredulously.

Jim shifted in his chair, his gaze averted.

"It's too little, too late," Walker said. He strode across the room to stand before the older man and glared down at him. Lowering his voice to a raspy pitch, his words tumbled out at a furious pace. "How do you suppose I felt when I tried, after my mother's death, at twelve and thirteen and fourteen and on, every day of every year to please you—to earn your approval? How do you suppose it was for a boy, living with a bastard like you? I worked harder than anyone, learned all I could to become the best cowhand, the best horse trainer, the best of everything there is to be on a ranch, until finally I was the best—and in the end, you still belittled me!"

Jim squinted up, breathing heavily. "I know. I know, son—"

"Don't *son* me!" Walker exclaimed. "I was never a son to you. But I tried. I knew you hated Dennis sitting inside all the time. I knew you wanted a boy who could ride beside you, who liked open country, a good horse and the wind at his back as much as you did. Why didn't you give me back what I gave you, Jim? Why didn't you?''

Lifting a beseeching hand, Jim started to say something, stopped, then tried again. "You were good on the ranch, Walker. You did work hard. I was proud of you, even if I didn't say it.''

Walker scoffed, whirling on his boot heels and heading for the door. Once there, he stopped. "I don't want compliments now. Where were they fifteen years ago? A thirty-year-old man doesn't need encouragement, Jim. I know what I am and what I can do, in spite of you. But don't think you can go back now, say you're sorry and make up for those long, hopeless years.''

Walker paused, his breathing labored, staring at Jim and knowing such overwhelming anger, he actually had to squint through the red veil that was misting his vision. He didn't think he'd ever been this furious, even after years of suppressed fury.

To keep from strangling Jim, Walker thrust his shaking hands into his front jeans pockets. When his fingers touched a piece of slick paper, he realized he'd put the twenty-year-old photo of Jim's rustling activities into his pocket. He didn't know why he'd put it there, exactly. Probably just to look at it once more. To remind himself of the low-down, thieving scum his stepfather really was.

Jim was talking again, his voice sounding distant, as if coming from another room. Walker had to strain through his ricocheting thoughts to hear the words.

"...so I don't expect you to understand everything. I did the best I could...."

Again Walker's attention slipped. *The best he could?* He grimaced.

He fingered the photograph in his pocket and suddenly knew that now was the time. Today. This minute. He would pull out the picture and make his case. The satisfaction he'd get, watching big Jim face his worst nightmare, would be just revenge for all the years of pain and loneliness he'd endured because of the older man's selfishness.

Drawing it out of his pocket slowly, the better to savor his vengeance, Walker stared at Jim, who was still talking, trying fruitlessly to excuse his neglect. Didn't he know that there was no excuse?

Neither Jim nor Stacey seemed to have noticed the small picture in his palm. They were both too involved in trying to get him to forgive and forget. Ha!

Walker let his gaze linger on Stacey for a few final seconds. Even though his focus was on Jim, one part of him, even now, could see she was truly beautiful. Soft. Womanly. And a more giving person he'd never met. She made his blood sing, his heart hammer, and she stirred his imagination as no other ever had.

Producing his evidence and forcing Jim to change his will would thrust her from his life forever. She'd have to leave the ranch, take her boy with her.

The thought gave him pause. He'd grown attached to Geoff; the kid had an open, eager attitude he liked. Never before had Walker had the opportunity to give of himself as he had these past weeks. Without vanity, he knew his knowledge of horsemanship was vast—it was good to pass it on to a boy like Geoff. There was a deep satisfaction in the giving.

The photo in his hand burned against his skin.

For the first time he wondered if producing it would be worth the stormy upheaval that was sure to result. Would losing Stacey and, yes, Geoff be worth revenge?

Suddenly he was assailed with doubt.

"So what do you say, Walker?" Jim looked up from where he sat, slumped in his chair. At that moment Walker noticed the older man's pallor. It might be from the trauma of the horse's kick, but Jim didn't look so good. Without his perpetual, pearl-gray Stetson, it was evident that he was losing his hair—had already lost most of it, in fact—and his scalp was shiny and a bit pink on top.

Walker tried impatiently to shake off the observation. Everyone grew old.

But the skin around Jim's chin was getting jowly, and brown age spots dotted his once-taut face.

"Dammit," Jim said. "Why don't you say something, boy?"

Stacey was studying Walker closely. "Maybe you can't forget, Walker. But you could forgive. If you tried."

All at once Walker lost patience with his own weakness. He hated his inability to follow through with the action he'd dreamed of for years. He gritted his teeth. "I'll never forget. Nor forgive."

"All right." Stacey came around Jim's chair to stand before Walker. She reached up to lay a slim hand against his hard cheek. "But perhaps you could go on from here. You two can get out of this vicious circle of mutual abuse. You can try to live together peaceably. Respect each other."

Walker looked into her face and knew he would not be able to see his plan through. Alive in Stacey's eyes was trusting faith, an innocent belief that he would act honorably. She believed him a bigger man than he was, and he couldn't bear to let her down. He was accustomed to having her think of him as a worthy man. Worthy men, he knew, did not go in for petty revenge.

He grasped her hand with a deliberate movement and set it aside. Suddenly, he felt cast adrift. What should he do now if he couldn't forgive and couldn't compromise? How was he to handle life without the bitterness that had driven him for so long?

He couldn't accept Stacey's love, and he couldn't accept Jim's apology. There was no alternative: he'd have to leave the Bar M.

Chapter Eleven

Without a word Walker pivoted on his heels and started for his bedroom. Stacey followed. She sensed victory near—very soon she would be able to make Walker agree to put the past aside and live peaceably with Jim. And with her.

In his room, Walker strode to his closet, and Stacey watched, puzzled, while he pulled out an old canvas zipper bag, yanked open the pine chest of drawers and started stuffing clothing into the bag. Her certainty that he would come around began to wane. From her position in the doorway she asked, "Walker, what are you doing? Are you going somewhere?"

He didn't answer, his jaw so tense it looked wired shut. Movements jerky, he wasted no time folding the clothes, but shoved pants and shirts inside, zipped the case closed and then shouldered his way by Stacey to stride down the hall. She chased after him, peppering him with questions, finally hanging onto his arm.

"You have to stop," she said, panting. She'd known he was strong, but he shook her off like a horse shaking off a fly. Fear took hold and mounted inside her. He actually looked as if he meant to pack up and move out!

"Walker, wait!" As she followed, she caught a glimpse of Jim standing in the living room, morosely observing the scene with dead eyes. The older man made no move to stop Walker; he remained still, as if defeated. With no time to wonder at Jim's expression, she stumbled down the front steps and out into the daylight.

An unseasonable chilly wind swept over her bare arms, and an overhead cloud cover blocked the setting sun. She barely noticed. Again she grabbed Walker's arm.

At last he stopped in the barn doorway. When he glowered at her, she was amazed at the wild restlessness she saw vibrating in him. His voice was low, curt. "What do you want from me?"

She stared into his eyes, desperately seeking the man she loved who was hidden inside this frightening stranger. Swallowing hard, she said, "Peace. Harmony. I want to work with you, Walker, not against you."

He shook his head. "You won't have to worry about working with me. You've won. You can have the ranch." His tone flat, he finished, "I'm leaving."

Horrified, she gasped. "Leaving? For good?"

His silence was an eloquent answer.

"But what are you talking about?" Her fingers bit into his forearm again. "This was your mother's property. And her mother's before her and on back. You—you told me so yourself! You can't just leave."

"Watch me." With that he was swallowed by the shadows of the dark barn. In shock, she stood as if rooted to the spot. The cold wind picked up its pace, sent unfriendly gusts straight through her thin blouse and buffeted her hair against her numb cheeks. In less than a minute Walker

emerged with his silver-tooled saddle, hefting it by the horn.
In the bed of his battered pickup truck, he settled his canvas bag and his saddle.

For the life of her she couldn't speak. Standing beside the
truck now, he hesitated. Something flickered in his eyes, and
it appeared to Stacey almost as if he were taking pity on her.
"Don't worry. I'll start over, make my own way someplace
else." From his jeans pocket he extracted what looked to be
an old photograph, although from her vantage point, and
in the fading light, she couldn't see it well.

Staring at it intently, Walker drew a deep, difficult breath
and let it out in a quick burst. She watched, confused, as he
systematically began to rip the picture into tiny shreds, then
let them blow away in the breeze.

She didn't know what the photo was, nor did she care. All
she knew was that Walker actually meant to forsake the
ranch...and her. And all for the sake of his ridiculous pride!

Before she could say anything more, he captured her gaze,
his own both reckless and hunted. "Goodbye, Stacey." He
turned to climb into the cab.

"I didn't think," she started slowly, her voice trembling,
"that Margaret had raised any cowards."

He stopped with one leg inside. "What?"

"You, Walker, taking the cowardly way out." She twisted
her hands before her and prayed for the right words.

He grimaced. "It's the only way."

"No." Her voice quavered, and she strove to steady it.
"What will happen to the Bar M if you go? What will become of the wild horses you profess to love so much? Who
will protect them?"

His slashing brows lifted a fraction, then settled back into
their customary scowl. "They'll survive," he growled. He
was inside the cab now, thrusting the key into the ignition.

"But what about me?" she cried, her reserve cracking.
She lurched forward to clutch the truck door.

He stared stonily ahead.

"You're a chicken," she tried to shout, and was furious when it came out only as a croak. Her throat felt tighter than it ever had, the knot that was building inside a burning thing. "You're afraid of one small woman, aren't you?" she accused. "It's not really the ranch you're escaping from, is it? And it's not your relationship with Jim. I know what you're feeling, Walker. I'm feeling it, too." She halted a brief moment, gathering courage.

She'd known. Oh, yes, she knew the truth. But Walker was still hiding from it—clouding the real issue with other, outside concerns. It took all her heart and soul for her to whisper, "You're afraid to love me. So you're running away. But you can't run from love, Walker. Don't you know that?"

Inside the cab he gunned the engine into life. She read his lips, more than heard his answer. "Maybe I can."

All at once she wanted to kick him, hit him, do anything to force him into realizing what a terrible mistake he was about to make. As surely as she knew the sun would set over the mountains, she knew that if he left, he would never return.

The fool. How dare he take something as rare and precious as a woman's love—*her* love—and throw it away?

"All right then. Go!" She spoke through clenched teeth. "You owe me nothing." She stepped back from his pickup, taking a quarter turn away from him. With her arms crossed tightly beneath her breasts, she asked the truck's hood ornament, "Will you wound a child with your selfishness?"

Walker frowned a question at her.

"Don't you think you should at least say goodbye to Geoff? He's terribly attached to you. It's going to hurt him, your leaving. You owe him a few words."

He considered that.

She knew she'd hit a nerve when he opened the door and got out, leaving the engine running. He nodded once. "I'll say goodbye to Geoff."

Watching him with eyes that ached, she forced herself to stand by the pickup and not follow him.

She almost laughed then. It was ironic, crazy. All the time she'd spent on the ranch, she'd worried that in some way Walker would force her to leave. If not because of his obvious dislike, then perhaps with the more insidious and far more dangerous threat of seduction. But things hadn't turned out that way. Somehow, everything had reversed itself, and she had been the one to run *him* off.

Her eyes filmed over, and she shivered in the cold. As quickly as it had come, her anger seeped away. Dully, she studied Walker's bag and saddle in the bed of his truck. Almost without thinking, she leaned over and grabbed the bag, then the saddle, groaning with the effort to lift them out. Setting them behind the truck, she waited for Walker's return. Taking his things didn't make sense, like standing before a band of stampeding mustangs and shouting "Whoa!"

It was stupid. But it made her feel better.

On the way to the horse pasture to say a difficult goodbye to the boy he'd begun to think of as his own, Walker searched for words to explain why he would never see Geoff again. He came up empty.

The corral rails he'd helped build at age fourteen still stood stout and strong. The barn they'd put in when he was twenty-two loomed large and useful. It protected sick or weak stock, housed the horses, equipment, hay. The cowboys had celebrated its raising by getting as drunk as hoot owls. Walker's lips quirked in a fleeting smile. He'd been one of them.

The mountains and meadows visible from where he stood were rough, wild country, yet they were green and alive and beautiful. He sighed. Leaving his family heritage would be the hardest thing he'd ever do in his entire life.

No. In a heartbeat Walker realized that was wrong. Leaving the dark-haired woman with the unusual blue eyes—that would be the hardest. He'd miss her unbearably. Stacey had made him smile, a feat few others had accomplished. How often he'd forgotten his bitterness around her.

Walker dropped his gaze to the hard-packed earth and his hands fisted. Dammit! She wanted too much from him! She wanted him to compromise—give in like a damn lapdog.

The entire situation was impossible.

Why should he share the ranch with anyone? Morally, it was already his. Unfortunately, legally, it was not. And Jim, the two-legged coyote, deserved to suffer, if Walker's leaving could induce any such emotion. So the best thing to do would be to follow through with his plan. Walker straightened his shoulders. He'd made up his mind, he'd keep it. Strong men did not waver from decisions.

He would go. Now.

Quickening his steps, he rounded the barn. Shadows gathered at the base of the building, making shapes indistinct. It took him several seconds to understand what was going on: Geoff was inside the forbidden corral, half lying across Ridgefire's back. The boy crooned softly to the fierce animal, who stood quietly, even bending his neck and twisting to nose the boy's arm with tentative affection.

Walker gaped. He stifled his first reaction to rush in and grab Geoff before the unpredictable stallion exploded. Something in the boy's demeanor gave him pause. Geoff was calm, relaxed, comfortably stretched over the horse's back. He stroked the burr-filled mane, and Walker could see the animal enjoyed the attention.

The mares grazed quietly nearby, and two six-month-old colts frolicked close to them. All was calm.

He must have made a noise, because Geoff lifted his head and spotted him by the gate. The boy slid off and after a last pat on the horse's neck, approached. He eyed the older man solemnly. "Am I in trouble?"

"Trouble?" Walker echoed, feeling stunned by the trust he'd seen between boy and horse. At that moment something inside him was born. He didn't know what it was, exactly, dizzily closing his eyes against the revelation, but it was uplifting. Good.

"You told me never to come into the corral," Geoff went on. "But Ridgefire and I..." He gestured toward the horse.

Walker opened his eyes and said the obvious. "You're friends."

The boy nodded. "You told me it'd take care and patience. You said even a rank outlaw can learn to trust again."

Awed, Walker caught his breath and put a hand to his chest. He wondered if a mule kick could shock him more. Suddenly he was ashamed of himself. Deeply, embarrassingly, stunningly ashamed. Clutching the weathered wood of the gate, he studied the peeling paint as if it were the most interesting thing in the world.

He thought of Jim, who'd extended a hand, and had asked for forgiveness. He thought of Geoff, persevering until he'd triumphed with the aloof stallion. Lastly he thought of Stacey, proudly attempting to convince him that love could conquer all.

Would his damnable pride make him lose everything he held dear? Stacey had called him a coward. Now he admitted she was right. The hell of it was, it had taken a ten-year-old boy to show him.

* * *

Stacey saw Walker return from the horse pasture at a dead run. He didn't spare her a glance; he just threw himself into his truck, gunned the idling engine and jammed the gearshift into drive. She watched, speechless.

He stomped on the accelerator so hard, his rear wheels fishtailed in the gravel and dirt. Seconds later, he had disappeared.

While she hadn't expected a prolonged goodbye kiss, she hadn't thought he would simply charge into his pickup and fly off down the mountain hell-bent for leather.

But that was exactly what he'd done.

She stood in the dust, staring after him, her heart closing in on itself with the most searing pain she could ever imagine. Stacey was left alone.

She pressed a hand to her mouth. Would she never learn whom to trust and whom to suspect? Would she never mature enough to discern a deserving man from one who wasn't?

Tears gathered again as she stared into the direction that Walker had taken, toward Bakersfield—as if by keeping vigil, she could will him back. A swirl of dried leaves was the only evidence that he'd ever been there.

All her worry about the matter of trust was moot, she realized abruptly, hating her spilling tears. Because whether she'd decided to or not—wanted to or not—she'd given Walker her heart, anyway... and her trust.

Shoulders slumped, she turned toward the house. Hopelessness rose in her heart and threatened to choke her. Pain stabbed at her.

Walker, she cried inwardly, *I love you!*

She hadn't taken more than three stumbling steps when something caught her eye: Walker's bag and saddle. He'd been in such a hurry, he hadn't noticed she'd removed them. But she knew as surely as she knew her own name that he wouldn't leave behind his precious, silver-trimmed saddle. It might take him until he reached town, an hour and a half away, before he realized he didn't have them, but he would be back.

And when he returned, she'd be there, waiting.

Dropping to the ground, Stacey settled her back against the hard leather of the cantle and tried to get comfortable. With her knuckles she scrubbed at the last bit of moisture that had escaped from her eyes and lifted her chin. The stiff leather dug into her lower back, and she changed position four times, wondering how on earth cowboys managed to use these tough things for pillows.

She shrugged away her discomfort. It didn't matter if she got a little backache because it took Walker three hours to get to town and back; she wasn't about to budge. A guest wandered out and glanced at her curiously. From somewhere inside she manufactured a smile, then ignored him. Rudy could finish and serve dinner. She had this one final opportunity to change Walker's mind, and she wasn't about to find comfort elsewhere and take the chance of missing him. When he returned, he'd have to listen to her.

It did, indeed, take Walker three full hours to get to Bakersfield and back. Beside him on the seat sat his purchase, and he kept checking it to make sure that, as he drove the final turns before he reached the ranch, it didn't fall onto the floorboards and become damaged. Outside, it was quite dark, with a bright moon overhead the only illumination for the wood-burned sign that read The Bar M.

He'd never expected to find Stacey sitting calmly where he'd left her, reclining in the moonlight and propped, surprisingly, against his saddle. He flicked a quick glance into the bed of his truck, just now realizing that she must have removed his things. He hadn't even known they were gone.

Stacey offered him so much; she'd even made the heroic admission that she loved him. At least he thought that was what she'd meant. For these three long hours, Walker had felt deep chagrin; she had been braver than he had.

Shrugging, he drove eagerly toward her, slammed on the brakes and jumped out. He'd been ashamed of his cowardice, but no more. Now, it was his turn to take a chance, gamble on a gut feeling—on what he truly wanted in life—and leave mistrust and false pride behind.

Her dark hair was blowing around her head, and in the lamplight from the house he could see that her cheeks were pink from windburn. She looked cold; goose bumps were rising on her arms. In all his life he didn't think he'd ever seen a prettier picture.

He grabbed his purchase, hid it behind his back and hurried toward her.

"Hello, Walker," she said pleasantly from her position on the ground. Her tone was polite enough, but her small fist was clenched around the latigo strap as if clutching a lifeline. And in her pretty eyes shone a steely determination he'd rarely seen. "I knew you'd be back for your precious saddle. But I'm afraid I won't let you have it until you admit one thing."

"What's that, honey?" he asked gently. His damn hands, clutching the flowers behind his back, were shaking. He swallowed hard. He had the terrifying notion that time was running out, that he had to capture Stacey now while he still had a chance. He took a step closer and held out the chrysanthemums. She took them and hugged them in her arms.

"Now you'll have to admit," she said, allowing him to pull her to her feet, "that you and I are in love." Unblinking, she stared at him. He had the impression she was holding her breath. That was okay. He was having trouble himself in getting air into his lungs.

"All right," he said with a grateful smile, his heart expanding until it brimmed. "We're in love."

Her eyes widened. "You—you admit it?" she sputtered.

The pink blooms glowed, but nothing could match the beautiful shade of Stacey's cheeks. Despite his best efforts, a few of the stems had broken on the long drive. He fingered one snapped stalk. "I know these aren't perfect, but... I guess what I want to say is... maybe I *can* give flowers. To you."

Deep in her eyes he read the wonder he felt in himself. They stared at each other for long moments, and he knew that through Geoff, a boy wise beyond his years, he had learned that even a confirmed cynic can begin to trust again.

"If you want," he began carefully, hoping to get out his rehearsed speech before she could say more, "if you want to make changes on the Bar M, or even control it, I don't care." She gasped, but he pressed on. "What's important in life isn't my pride, but you. I—I want to come home to you at night. And I want to help raise Geoff. He's a great kid." Was he jabbering like a rummy old-timer? "So..." He hesitated a long time, forcing himself to breach the barrier of insecurity and fear with thoughts of all he could gain. "So, will you have me?" He touched the bump on his nose. "Even the parts that aren't perfect?"

Stacey swayed on her feet, and he grasped her by the elbows to steady her, waiting for what seemed interminable seconds. She glanced down at the flowers in her arms, crushing them between her fingers. He watched her swallow with difficulty. She spoke slowly, without inflection, as if afraid of his answer. "I can't live in a house with such dissension. Can you and Jim resolve your differences?"

He smiled. For her he'd take up bull riding, move to the city, give up horses. "I'll try, if he does."

"Walker," she warned.

"All right. I'll get along with him. For you. Besides, he as good as asked for my forgiveness. I guess I can give it."

"Good!" Jim boomed behind them from the doorway, startling them. A grinning Geoff stood at his side. Cheery light spilled out behind them. Jim went on, "I'll take it. Now get yourself unwrapped from that female, son. There'll be plenty of opportunity for that after the nuptials. It's high time now we made some plans for the ranch."

Walker wrapped an arm about Stacey's waist and held her to his side. "Plans? With each of us having equal say?"

"A'course!" Jim bellowed.

"Fine." Walker grasped Stacey by the wrist and quite forcefully towed her through the barn doorway, into an empty stall. He shut the door firmly behind them, then set aside the flowers. His arms closed around her with a measure of possessiveness he'd never before experienced. Thrilling him, she came to him instantly and offered up her lips. He took the offering, kissing her with all the pent-up love and tender passion he had in him.

The long years of habitual bitterness fell away. Walker knew now that Stacey alone had gradually replaced it with her laughter and her love. He sent up a quick but fervent prayer of thanks that some greater power had seen fit to send her into his life.

Her slender body pressed against his felt wonderfully sexy, magically right. She was chilled through, but he wasn't concerned. He planned to go on warming her for years. For the rest of his life.

"Oh, Walker," Stacey breathed, burying her face in his neck. "I don't know why you changed your mind about leaving. The reasons aren't important. I'm just so glad you didn't throw our love away." She pulled back an inch. "You had me so scared!"

He grinned sheepishly. "Me, too."

She threw a mock punch at his jaw, a punch he easily caught. Drawing her hand to his lips, he pressed a kiss on the leaping pulse at her wrist. "Even if I did leave, I'd just turn right back around. I could never stay away from you."

Moving slowly, Walker flattened her small hand against his chest. "I never figured to say this to a woman—but it's true. I love you. You have my heart, honey. Take care of it."

Stacey's eyes were wider and bluer than he'd ever seen them. Even lovelier than before. "I'll take care of you. You can trust me." She said the last words passionately, pressing her palm over his heart as if to protect it always.

He smiled, loving her more than he'd ever believed it possible for a man to love a woman. He was awed and humbled that he—a scarred, embittered man—had managed to win her heart.

Deep, deep contentment blazed through him.

"Will you really be my wife?" he asked against her lips.

Her mouth trembled as she smiled at him. Reaching up, she ran loving fingers lightly down his face, stopping at the imperfection on the bridge of his nose. "I'd marry you today, Wild Horse Walker," she pledged. "And one more thing."

"Yes?"

"I *love* this bump on your nose."

* * * * *

**HE'S MORE THAN
A MAN, HE'S
ONE OF OUR**

ONE MAN'S VOW
Diana Whitney

Single father Judd Tanner had his hands full with a houseful of
boys and one orphaned goddaughter. But a woman's touch
was the last thing he wanted. Women, he knew, were experts
at one thing—leaving. It didn't matter to Judd that from the
moment she'd arrived, Leslie Leighton McVay had his boys
behaving and his godchild smiling. It would take more than
that to convince him that the pretty drifter was really home
to stay....

Find out just what it takes for Judd to love again, in
Diana Whitney's ONE MAN'S VOW, available in June.

Fall in love with our **Fabulous Fathers**—and join the
Silhouette Romance family!

Silhouette
R O M A N C E™

Take 4 bestselling love stories FREE

Plus get a FREE surprise gift!

Special Limited-time Offer

Mail to Harlequin Reader Service®

3010 Walden Avenue
P.O. Box 1867
Buffalo, N.Y. 14269-1867

YES! Please send me 4 free Silhouette Romance® novels and my free surprise gift. Then send me 6 brand-new novels every month, which I will receive months before they appear in bookstores. Bill me at the low price of $1.99* each plus 25¢ delivery and applicable sales tax, if any.* I understand that accepting the books and gift places me under no obligation ever to buy any books. I can always return a shipment and cancel at any time. Even if I never buy another book from Silhouette, the 4 free books and the surprise gift are mine to keep forever.

215 BPA AJCL

Name _____

(PLEASE PRINT)

Address _____ Apt. No. _____

City _____ State _____ Zip _____

This offer is limited to one order per household and not valid to present Silhouette Romance® subscribers.
*Terms and prices are subject to change without notice. Sales tax applicable in N.Y.

USROM-93   ©1990 Harlequin Enterprises Limited

INTIMATE MOMENTS®
10TH
Anniversary

Celebrate our anniversary with a fabulous collection of firsts....

The first Intimate Moments titles written by three of your favorite authors:

NIGHT MOVES	**Heather Graham Pozzessere**
LADY OF THE NIGHT	**Emilie Richards**
A STRANGER'S SMILE	**Kathleen Korbel**

Silhouette Intimate Moments is proud to present a FREE hardbound collection of our authors' firsts—titles that you will treasure in the years to come, from some of the line's founding writers.

This collection will not be sold in retail stores and is available only through this exclusive offer. Look for details in Silhouette Intimate Moments titles available in retail stores in May, June and July.

SIMANNR

 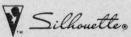

Silhouette Romance celebrates June brides and grooms and *You're Invited!* Be our guest as five special couples find the magic ingredients for happily-*wed*-ever-afters! Look for these wonderful stories by some of your favorite authors...

WED

Silhouette
R O M A N C E™

SMYTHESHIRE, MASSACHUSETTS.

Small town. Big secrets.

Silhouette Romance invites you to visit Elizabeth August's intriguing small town, a place with an unusual legacy rooted deep in the past....

THE VIRGIN WIFE (#921) February 1993
HAUNTED HUSBAND (#922) March 1993
LUCKY PENNY (#945) June 1993
A WEDDING FOR EMILY (#953) August 1993

Elizabeth August's SMYTHESHIRE, MASSACHUSETTS—
This sleepy little town has plenty to keep you up at night.
Only from Silhouette Romance!
